HOT VIKINGS - VOLUME 1

THE JÜRGENSEN VIKINGS

PEYTON LAWSON

Edited by Rachael Lammie
Cover by Peyton Lawson

BEACHES AND TRAILS
PUBLISHING

ABOUT THE AUTHOR

Peyton Lawson writes Steamy Historical Viking Romance. Her edge-of-your-seat action and adventure stories feature strong, fearless characters who always get their HEA.
She enjoys reading and traveling.

For updates on book releases, book recommendations, Viking Trivia, Sales, and GIVEAWAYS, subscribe to her Newsletter!

www.peytonlawsonromance.com

- facebook.com/peytonlawsonromance
- x.com/plawson_romance
- instagram.com/peytonlawsonromance
- amazon.com/author/peytonlawsonromance
- bookbub.com/authors/peyton-lawson
- tiktok.com/@Tiktok.com@peytonlawsonbooks

ALSO BY PEYTON LAWSON

SÖREN

HEALED BY A HIGHLAND WITCH

PROLOGUE

THE VESSEL CRESTED the waves teetering on the liquid precipice, suspended in a blackened sky.

Traces of white light, great fingers of fire wreathed the small ship in Thor's flames before it nosed down and plunged down the wall of water. The five men in the ship raced to the back of the craft. Two of them flung themselves out into the surf, holding the stern to keep the bow up. The boat's bottom smacked the waves, a vicious crack that rivalled the echoing thunder. The three men in the hull pulled their brothers back into the ship.

All five brothers broke to the oars, wading through ankle-high water on the deck. The ship was wallowing in the surf, and the storm raged on around them.

Abjörn stood, his sharp eyes seeing through the gloom in an almost uncanny way. He thrust his arm and yelled, but the sounds were lost in the teeth of the squall. His brothers understood, though. He had spotted land.

Tired cheers erupted. Hope set them moving with a lighter step though exhausted. The coast was unfamiliar, and the only certainty was that they had been blown off course. Where the Danish settlement was on the foreign shore was a good question. Still, at the moment, any shore was an excellent place to put in until they could empty the boat and wait out the storm.

Five giant Danes, each with arms enlarged with muscles built from rowing, set to the benches again and began to pull against the swell of the waves. After reaching the edge of the shore, the waves started to help, and powerful arms and chests tore the floundering boat through the last of the waves.

As soon as Sören felt the boat slide onto the sand, he jumped out, braving the crashing waves and pelting rain. He ran to the rocky shore, pulling the thick rope behind him and securing it to a tree that danced under the fierce winds.

His brothers jumped out, and between them, they managed to beach their craft and pulled furs and hides from the bottom for shelter as the fury of Thor ground itself against the foreign lands so far from home. Whether this was Scotland or somewhere else altogether remained to be seen. Right now, it did not matter, so long as they had a place to wait out the storm.

They ate to survive; a bit of cheese, some hard smoked meats. There would be enough to tide them over until the storm passed. The brothers huddled together under the tree line, staying as dry as the gods decreed, and waited.

The storm didn't last long. At midnight, the sky relented, and Odin called a halt to Thor's madness. The stars reappeared, a million fiery eyes curious to see the damage wreaked on fragile men.

In silence, they worked to bail the seawater from the bowels of the craft, anxious to meet the morning tide. They talked little, though still found time to laugh when the youngest stumbled and had to be fished out of the waves. An hour past dawn, the tide would be at its highest, and they could slip away from the shores and follow the coast to the new colony and begin to carve a life there.

The ship was put to rights under a baleful moon, a gibbous reminder of Hel and her kingdom of the unglorified dead. Exhausted and hurting from their battle with the sea, the brothers fell to the bottom of the craft and slept a few precious hours before the sun broke the horizon and they could sail once more.

As his brothers lay under their wet furs, breathing even and dreaming of glory, Sören woke with the discomforting feeling that all was not well. He rose and sat on the rowing bench, but the only sounds were the slow susurrus of the sea as it caressed the shore in apology for its temper tantrum.

Sören rose and slipped over the side of the boat and climbed up the beach. He headed for the trees, loosening his britches as he walked, needing to relieve himself. He'd gotten halfway to the thick trees and had only loosened his belt when he heard a sound.

In the darkness, something moved. A motion to his left caught his eye, a reflection in the pale moonlight. Another. These were not the sounds of nature, not wolves daring the sands and the smell of men. These were men, and as he turned, trying to act as though he were blind and stupid. He could see them.

The Viking longship had often made land on these shores enough for the locals to fear the dragon's prow. The Danes prided themselves that no village was a match for a raiding party, and so that was true. Still, he and his four brothers did not constitute a raiding party, and the Scots who surprised them had numbers and stealth on their side.

Not wanting to raise the alarm too obviously, Sören strolled casually to the prow and leaned on it as though he hadn't a care in the world. However, his heart was racing, the battle rage already coming upon him. He turned, acting casually, and set his shoulder to the boat. Sören shoved it as hard as he could, bellowing a war cry to wake his brothers, calling for them to dig in and help push the reluctant craft into the water.

Four heads rose from the inside of the ship as the villagers broke cover. They came at the vessel waving axes and hay forks and the occasional rusted sword, family heirlooms ill-maintained.

Sören gave the last heave as the four men in the boat readied their weapons, and the light, quick craft found her sea legs and began to draw out with the tide.

"ROW!" he screamed at his brothers, "There are too many, ROW!"

He splashed into the water after the ship. He only needed to reach and heave himself over into the protection of the wooden walls and help man the oars sent into the waves.

He did not get the chance.

Something hard and heavy hit him in the back of his head like a falling anvil. He heard his older brother calling his name, and then he only remembered floating, giving back to the sea. His last thought was for his brothers and their safety. That and standing in judgment before Odin.

Was being killed by a rock while running away worthy of Valhalla?

He waited in the sudden darkness for the Valkyrie and prayed for a quick release to her arms.

CHAPTER 1

FIRTHA THREW another log on the blaze and cast a wary glance upwards as the wind howled anew. "Father God, if ye be there, let the roof stay where it was placed."

A part of her was unsure if she was allowed to pray anymore, or indeed if she ever was. The wrath of Odin was undoubtedly on them now. To say she was responsible for the storm that savaged her little hut was as stupid as saying she was responsible for the fury of the Northmen. They raided the coasts and vanished again in their terrifying ships.

No one ever said that noblemen were above being stupid.

Thunder crashed through the swaying trees like a dragon from legend, dragging lightning behind it. The sky lit with fire that touched the tops of trees and sent them off, exploding slivers of wood and flame quenched by the torrential rains.

Firtha set the kettle over the flame, the rabbit boiling with the few vegetables she had been able to scrounge so early in the spring. Her mother had left her little enough before she died, but a knowledge of what was safe and what was poison was vital to a young woman living in the woods alone.

The door blew open. For a moment, she thought to blame the storm and hastened to fasten it again. Instead, she was pushed almost immediately back into the room as a figure from her nightmares entered her tiny shack. He ducked to pass the lintel; his shoulders were too broad to get through the frame. He staggered in, right side first, the side that held the great axe in a massive fist.

Firtha shrieked and scrabbled away from the newcomer, realizing suddenly the folly of having only a single door upon the crude dwelling. The stranger stood blocking the only way out, fingers of white fire tracing through the sky behind him like a spiderweb of light. He was nearly as tall as her roof, as broad as her table, and drenched by the rain. His furs were matted and clung to his frame, his boots shod, and his partly shaved head looked nearly out of place on shoulders as broad as her broomstick was long.

He looked around at the small hovel, the bed with clean rushes in the corner, the bright fireplace in brave defiance of the late winter storm, and the young woman tending the stew pot.

Firtha recoiled and pressed herself against the wall; the curses, threats, and lies she told to stay alive died on her lips. She forgot her reputation as a witch and fell to the ground in fear of the most primal giant male she'd ever seen.

He looked at her and smiled. Well, maybe not smiled. The expression upon his face twisted about, more like a grimace than anything. He bared his teeth, lifted that impossible ax in his hand…

…and promptly fell over like a cut oak.

The hut trembled as he hit the floor, taking down her simple table and reducing the furniture to so much firewood. Firtha stared, barely daring to breathe.

Was he dead? He certainly looked it, lying where he was, in the rubble and splinters. A shame too, given his well-muscled form. Though his features were hard, there was a pleasantness as to the set of his mouth, the placement of his eyes. Had he not been so terrifying, she might have been…intrigued?

Such nonsense. The storm raged through the open door, a spatter of rain upon her face reminding her where she was. One did not fall for fallen Vikings and as far as she could tell, this particular giant did not seem inclined to move. In fact, it almost seemed as if he were snoring.

CHAPTER 2

THERE WAS A DRAFT. Sören Jurgenson felt it first on his arm. He was warm and dry and comfortable, but a line of cool air along his flesh was actually a bit chilly. He tried to ignore it, to stay in the warmth and the soft comfort of wherever he was, but the longer he stayed without moving, the colder the wind blew over his flesh.

Awareness was slow to return. There was something about where he was that didn't feel right. For one thing, his bed at home was long enough that his feet didn't drape over the end. It was wider too. If he was abed, which he was starting to think he was, this one was too narrow, and the sides were pressing against his shoulders.

Besides, wasn't his bed was a long way away in Denmark?

Well, that woke him quick enough.

His senses heightened, and he cracked an eye, ready to spring from the bed and into whatever fight awaited him. Only nothing seemed familiar, and he was decidedly alone. He kept his eyes closed and pretended to sleep if anyone was watching; he could not see. In the meantime, he strained to hear even the slightest sound to tell him where he was.

Oddly enough, the first thing he heard was a woman singing. She had a passible voice, the song one he hadn't heard before. The language was whatever gibberish the Scots spoke. Recognizing this brought back other memories. The trek to the settlement. Being grounded.

His brothers…where were they?

He could no longer afford to lay about waiting to find out. He cracked an eyelid open just enough to take stock of his surroundings. He saw a small home, a shack really, though in good repair. He was lying in a bed in one corner of the small space, and across from him, something bubbled in a pot set in the fireplace. Whatever it was, it smelled wonderful, and his belly reminded him how long it had been since he'd eaten.

As he watched the door open, the rather pleasing form of a woman came in carting several logs, a dusting of snow on her shoulders. These she dumped near the fire, pausing to check what was in the pot. Satisfied, she bent to feed sticks to the fire, her skirts moving to outline a shapely backside. She was still singing, looking for all the world as though she were crooning to the flames as though it were a favoured pet. Coaxing it maybe, cajoling it to burn brighter perhaps. A touch of witchcraft?

He could only see her back, but her hair was black and had no streaks of grey, so she was likely young, a sight which raised more questions than it answered.

As she was staring at the fire, he took a chance and opened his eyes fully to take in the rest of the cottage, though in truth he would much rather have continued watching her. He forced himself to focus, remembering his first duty lay in figuring out just where he was. Girls with pleasing forms could wait, at least until he got his bearings.

It was a plain enough home, and took no time at all to examine. There were two chairs off to the side of the room, but notable. The walls were timber lashed together, and wattle and daub mixed in to fill the cracks. It had crumbled in some places, which accounted for the draft along his arm. It was a wonder the place did not fall down around them.

"Ye be awake," she spoke without turning around as though she had eyes in the back of her head. She stood in a lithe, sinuous movement. "Ye may call me Firtha."

For a moment, Firtha was silhouetted by the flames. Sören was mesmerized by the figure he saw through the cloth of her dress. He had been correct in thinking her backside was firm and round. As she turned, he saw the rest lived up to the promise of that first glance. Her hips were rounded and generous, but her legs...her legs were long and shapely, a masterwork of feminine beauty, and that was only from the shadows. He could well imagine such legs wrapped around him, the cries she would make in her ecstasy.

She turned and looked at him with no trace of fear. With her hair loose around her face in waves that cascaded to her shoulders, she might have been Idun herself, who only took this form that she might bring him back to life. If so, she had succeeded for he felt a stirring within his loins at the sheer sight of her. She was slender, her breasts high but not too large. In short, she was the most beautiful woman he'd ever seen, and his body ached for her. He was glad suddenly for the furs which covered him. Though he felt no shame in being naked, such a revealing reaction to his nurse and saviour would likely not be appreciated.

She crossed to him in the small room and knelt by the bed, leaning over him to rest a hand upon his forehead. "Yer fever broke in the night. Is yer head better?"

He tried to speak, but the only sound he could utter was a cough. His throat was parched, and the violent action took the last of his energy with it. Yet, while his body was weak, the part that had responded to her silhouette was getting harder to ignore. Her hand was rough with callouses as she slid her palm over his forehead, but it was warm and strong. He ached to feel that hand on other parts of him, imagining the reaction such fingers could tease from him.

By the gods, this woman must have cast a spell over him to give him such awareness of her form.

She turned and produced a cup of water. It was clean and pure and cold, and he sipped it gratefully. "Better," he managed to croak out. Then it struck him. "You speak Danish."

"Good thing too," She smiled at him and set the cup down on the floor. It was clear she had no intention of explaining how she had come to know his language.

"How did I get here?"

She sighed and arranged her skirts around her as she rose. "All I know is, ye came crashing through my door and dropped yerself through my table. It was a decent piece of furniture, at least while it lasted." She shot him a look he couldn't interpret, but there was a great deal of humour in her eyes.

"I'm naked." It sounded trite, but the more he was around her, the more it mattered. If she wanted him, she only needed to climb in with him. He tried to reach for her all the same, but his arms would not obey the command properly and fell against the furs which covered him. He tried a different approach, one that did matter more than others. "I need to find my brothers, to be sure they're…." He tried to sit up, his robust frame making the bed groan under his weight. The furs slid down his chest and pooled in his lap.

The room swam, the heat of the fire felt like the flames of the Christian Hell, and he fell back against the straw-filled mattress. One of the straps that held the mattress in place gave under him but didn't break.

The woman's look was one of concern as she bent over him again, her deft hands mending the bandage around his head. He tried not to look at the bodice that had seen better days and was becoming threadbare. He was no match for this manner of witchery though. Her nipples made two pleasing marks on the cloth, and the way the thin material clung to her only increased his desire for her.

Helpless. I am helpless before her.

All the same, it was a lovely sight to see before drifting off to sleep. His dreams were haunted by the black-haired vixen with rounded hips, pert breasts, and laughing eyes.

CHAPTER 3

THANK Odin he fell back onto the bed. It had been a feat of some hours to get him off the floor the first time. If he'd landed there again, she wasn't sure she was up to the task.

The fur had slipped down as he tried to sit up, and even though he'd been confined to her bed for nearly a fortnight, he hadn't wasted away in that time. His chest was still as broad as her cot, and his shoulders even more so. There was muscle under that skin, hard, solid muscle, and he had just enough chest hair to play with, but not so much that he could be mistaken for an animal in the dark.

She rebandaged what he'd torn when he tried to stand. The injury on his hip was bleeding again, though it wasn't as bad as it was. Ironically, he'd survived whatever had created a crater in the back of his head, walked to her cottage in a thunderstorm, and yet somehow had sustained a wound by falling on her table.

Well, no one said Vikings were graceful. Lusty to be sure, for she had seen that with her own eyes when he'd awakened and made no pretence for the way he'd stared at her. But never graceful.

She shook her head as she bent again to her task. To tend the wound, she'd had to remove the clothing from his hips. To her surprise, it had become harder to maintain what her mother would call a "healer's distance" the more time she spent with him. When she'd undressed him purely to tend his wounds and get him out of the wet clothing he wore, she'd fought hard to maintain that professional distance.

She shook her head at her own foolishness now as she reached across him to replace the bandage over the fresh dressing, she'd given him. She could feel the blush in her face as she tended the wound and whipped the furs over him again as quickly as possible. It was easier to ignore his attraction to her when the evidence wasn't poking at her. My, but he had a way about him of coming to attention when she was near. Even unconscious, he seemed to crave her touch and moaned in ways that made her blood thrill when she'd accidentally come into contact with the hardened flesh.

It made her wonder how he would sound if she grasped him fully in her hand.

She sighed a little as she tucked this most intriguing bit of flesh back out of sight. A woman ought not to have such a fascination for such things. Her mother had declared such equipage as the surest way a woman could find trouble. Firtha already had more than her fair share of that, thank you very much.

She was not so cruel, however, as to cover his chest. She gave herself that much pleasure. His stomach was flat, and the muscles along his rib cage and over his chest and shoulders told of a lifetime of hard work. His hand seemed equally capable and strong. Where they capable of gentleness too? Or would he only know how to be rough? Was he the brutal conqueror everyone said the Danes were?

She ran her hands over his chest, telling herself she was checking for any broken or bruised ribs. Of course, by now she knew he had no such injuries there. Maybe this was more for her own pleasure after all. She blushed and gave a business-like check under his eyelids to be sure he was unconscious. Only then did she wipe her hands on her skirt. The sensation of her own palms upon her thighs, mixed with the image of what lay beneath the furs, made her mouth go dry.

Oh, if he would only wake and touch her for himself...

Seeing as how he was not inclined to do so anytime soon, she hiked her skirt, just enough to let her right hand slide up her leg and touch herself. She let her eyes wander over him as he lay there, his chest rising and falling in the peaceful throes of sleep. She decided that he had a strong face but a gentle one. The lines around his eyes hinted at a life of laughter. The muscular build had likely been carved by hard work and pain. He was a virile specimen worth daydreaming about. Her fingers parted and spread herself open. She ached for something she couldn't put a name to, throbbing with need, leaving her breathless as she touched herself almost hesitantly. What was she doing?

Nothing. I am doing nothing wrong. I am just…

Forget justification. She wanted what she wanted, let that be enough. Already she breathed harder, her fingers pressing just there as she watched his strong hands. She slowly pulled one onto her other arm; his fist would quickly wrap around her forearm. She returned to her ministrations and felt the heat flowing through her.

She became so lost in her own mind, with the passions of her touch filling her mind, that she nearly screamed when his hand clasped around her arm. As she thought, he fully swallowed her wrist in his hand. She pulled her fingers from under her skirt and hid that hand behind her. Had he seen? Did he know what she had done?

She pulled gently, and the hand slipped off of her arm and fell on his chest.

Wait. He wasn't even awake?

She peeled back an eyelid to check. He never so much as moved.

He hadn't noticed what she'd been doing. She was sure of it. Mostly sure of it. The dratted ship's mast he seemed to be trying to hide under the blanket was no indication; it hadn't shrunk at all, and she doubted it could grow any more than it already had.

She pulled the furs up to his chin and let him deal with whatever discomfort his body might be giving him. She was only tending his wounds, after all. Whatever other issues he had, were none of her business, plain and simple.

She stood and turned to the cottage window, the one her mother was so proud of. It had real glass, even though the pane was warped and cloudy. The first traces of snow tumbled across her field of vision, sticking to the denuded branches of the nearest trees, which had waited breathlessly for their winter coat for the past two weeks. A new problem forming, for once winter set in, they would be trapped her together. Her body, still aching from unspent passion, trembled. She told herself it was the cold which made her shake so. The truth trembled at the cusp of her thoughts.

So, I have a Viking all my own. Can I keep him?

It was enough to be considered a witch. Afraid of being turned to stone, the villagers kept their distance. The local priest had been decrying her from the pulpit, and her clients had thinned out, preferring to suffer rather than submit to Satan's remedies.

But to have a Viking for a pet? A stranded Dane? She'd heard the local Lord had given a significant part of his holding to the Danes by order of the king. It was part of the Danegeld, the extortion money paid to the Danes to leave the rest of the kingdom intact. She was already in the Lord's disfavour; harbouring a man such as this would only condemn her further.

"They can only burn me once," she told a passing snowflake. She turned and looked back at her pet Viking. "Might as well enjoy the life I have now...."

She returned to kneeling at his bedside and lay her head upon the broad chest. His heart was fierce, and the thudding against her cheek soothed her.

"All right, I'll enjoy this life after he wakes up."

She dozed lightly, kneeling on the dirt floor, the blazing fire keeping the chill at bay, her head rising and falling with each new breath he took.

I have my own Viking.

It was a most exciting thought.

CHAPTER 4

THE LIGHT HAD AT LEAST BECOME bearable. It no longer hurt to open Sören's eyes, though he did so cautiously. The girl was still there, sitting in a chair and carving something he couldn't see. Not carving, he realized, peeling. She was dutifully peeling and cutting the tiny potato before dropping it into the kettle that hung over the fire.

His stomach announced that it hadn't been filled in a long time. It felt as though his belly button was going to fall inward from lack of food. The rumble of hunger was loud enough for her to hear it from across the room. She turned and smiled at him.

"How be ye?"

It was the same voice he remembered from before. He'd thought he'd dreamed her. How much of what he remembered was a fevered fantasy, and how much was a genuine memory?

He was still naked; that much hadn't changed.

"Hungry." He tested his voice but found it working well. "There's a draft in this house."

"There are several drafts in this house," she corrected him but didn't seem upset by his observation. "I patch them as I can, but lately, I've been occupied by something else." She grinned at him, her face lit up. It was as if the sun had come out. "I've not slept in my bed for a couple of weeks now."

"Weeks?" He sat up quickly and caught himself with the edge of the cot. The room spun, but only for a moment, and then he was able to make sense of the world once more. "I've been here weeks?"

"Three, to be exact. Or rather, it will be three in two days." Her smile faded, "The injury to yer head was pretty bad. I've seen men die with wounds like yers."

He reached up automatically and touched the back of his head. The flesh was tender. He imagined the bone beneath felt a little soft, but nausea abated quickly, and the room had the decency to remain still. "I have to find my brothers." He swung his legs off the bed, much to her objections.

"Ye be far too big for me to put yer back in that bed again. I swear if ye fall down, yer sleeping wherever ye end up. I mean it."

Sören set his feet on the hard-packed ground. The chill of the draft might well have been coming from the dirt; his feet nearly froze on contact. He rested his elbows on his knees and hung his head until the little cabin settled down.

"Where are my clothes?"

She gave him a sour look. "They're in a box under the bed." She sniffed, "I needed to put it there so ye dinna fall through the bottom of the mattress."

He stood then. He was surprised when she turned away from him and focused on her fire so intently. She had been the one to undress him; indeed, she'd already seen him naked; why turn away now? Her modesty confused him and left him in no small way aroused. Such hiding meant she cared and saw him as more than a patient. Such thoughts pleased him.

He had to lift the small cot to get the box out from under it. It was true that he had stretched out the ropes that gave the structure for the mattress to lay on; he promised himself he would tighten that up before leaving.

He dressed quickly, though it was a pleasant surprise she'd cleaned his clothing. In Denmark, cleanliness was much prized. The trip across the sea and the ensuing chaos had left him and his clothes in a sad state. Apparently, she had done seen to both while he slept.

He slammed his foot into the boot as he finished dressing. The furs he typically wore as an outer covering were draped over the bed. The little house was too warm with the roaring fire to even consider putting them on. The heat made his head spin.

Or being up and about did. Sören sat heavily on the bed. He didn't want to admit it, but the simple act of getting dressed was almost more than he could handle.

She turned a little and saw he was dressed and took the kettle off of the fire using a thick cloth to save her hands. She set it on the hearth and ladled two bowls from the thick broth. Without a word, she handed one to him and tore a chunk of stale, hard bread and a wedge of cheese from a basket hanging from the rafters. Her fingers brushed his, long and delicate. Such tiny hands to have cared for him all this time.

He dipped the bread experimentally into the bowl and took a bite. The stew softened the hard bread, and his body responded to the food with a ravenous appetite. Before he realized he'd eaten, he was scraping the last of the stew from the bottom of the bowl with the remaining crust.

"Did ye even taste it?" She grinned at him, her eyes alight with laughter. Sören handed the bowl back to her and shrugged. "Do you not have a table?"

For some reason, the question seemed to be a cause for much merriment.

DESPITE HER CONCERN for an ailing patient, it was good to be back in her own bed. He'd tightened the cords that held the mattress, and she'd taken the straw-stuffed bag and beaten it within an inch of its life. The end result was the first good night's sleep she'd had since he broke down her door and landed on her table. If she lay awake at least part of that night, inhaling deeply of the masculine scent which clung to the bedding, it was no one's business but her own.

She woke at dawn, a lifetime of habit setting her internal cycle of rest, and looked to the floor where the giant had bedded down in his own furs. She'd put most of the rest of her cut firewood in or near the fire. At least he wouldn't freeze to death on her. On the other hand,

Vikings slept naked in the snow and found blizzards refreshing from what she'd heard.

She chastised herself for thinking of him naked again, and for worse, touching herself again as she did so. She really needed to let that image go, once and for all. In fact, maybe she should be getting up and tending to her unexpected guest rather than lying about thinking about him. She redirected her gaze to the floor where he should have been sleeping.

He wasn't there.

There were no furs. No clothing. No sign of Sören. She bolted upright in bed, a noise of dismay leaving her lips.

Winter had sunk its claws into the coast. Even the sea's salt spray had frozen on the trees, and ice wove spiderwebs out into the water. Even for a hale and healthy man, this was no time for travel. It didn't matter how accustomed he might be to the cold.

"He's not even completely healed!"

That she was talking to herself again seemed the final straw. She rose, ignoring the cold on her bare feet, and pulled her mother's shawl from the peg. She wrapped it around her, ready to run barefoot in the snow to find him if need be. He wasn't going out to die and ruin all her hard work.

In that instant, the door blew open with a bang, and he thundered in again. This time, he wasn't injured but staggered under a large armful of cut logs. He closed the door with his foot and saw her as he did.

"Good morning."

He smiled at her. A genuine, open smile. It was the first time she'd seen that on his face, and she decided she liked it. He looked less like a monster from legend and more like a mischievous boy who got caught out pretending to be a giant. That thought made her smile back, her shoulders relaxing as her panic subsided.

"Good morning."

"I got some firewood." He stood there holding what had to be nearly double her weight in wood. He made no move to put it down.

"I see that." She pointed to the edge of the hearth where the last two of her logs sat waiting their turn warming her cottage. "You can put that there."

He started as though he'd forgotten that he was holding enough firewood to last them most of a month. He dropped the wood and then bent to stack it neatly in a corner.

"The world is frozen," he said to the wood. "Ice and snow in my lands are...different." He paused and turned to face her. "I cannot find my people in this."

"No." Firtha agreed quickly. "No. The ice would tear up a boat if I had one to offer. Most of the passes through the hills are treacherous this time of year. The snow will likely melt, but then the fog comes and freezes. Men have become lost in their own yards when this happens."

He seemed to put the logs in place with a touch more force than necessary. "I need to stay until the winter passes." He held his hand over the last log added to the stack, and Firtha belatedly realized he was waiting for her permission.

"Of course." Though part of her rejoiced at holding onto him as long as she could, her more practical nature warned against harbouring an enemy of her Lord's. Not that the pompous old man cared for her anyway, but he wasn't openly hostile to her yet. She looked at the broad back and wide shoulders and decided the old Lord could go hang himself. With a boldness which surprised her, she lay a hand on the Dane's shoulder and whispered, "Ye be welcome here."

He seemed to cringe from her touch, though he certainly had shown interest in her before. He finished stacking the wood and stood. Firtha scrambled to her feet with him, unsure now that she had been reading the situation aright. Had his rather impressive display of interest solely been the result of some unconscious urge while mending? Embarrassed, she drew back, no longer sure what to say.

"I can fix yer table." He nodded to the door ad the scrap wood stacked against the side of the house. The scrap wood that used to be her table.

"Is it so bad?" She held her hands in front of her, not daring to touch him again.

"My brothers left me for dead." He looked overhead at something far beyond the walls of her home. "And now..." He gestured to the cabin and shrugged a rather impressive sight. She moved to comfort him, the healer instinct working independently, but he suddenly turned and refused to look at her. "I will start immediately." He spoke gruffly, his voice a low growl as he stared at her a long moment before bolting past her, right out the door again. Why he should be angry with her, she could not fathom. This was worse than disinterest.

Firtha stood dumbfounded in the middle of the single room, shivering from the draft Sören left in his wake. That's when she noticed her dress had slipped off her shoulder; she was uncovered from neck to shoulder, the swell of her breast prominently displayed.

He hadn't even reacted.

So be it then. She pulled the dress to rights and wondered at her own wantonness.

CHAPTER 5

FIRTHA ADDED a bit of spice to the meat, glad the work gave her something else to concentrate on for a spell. Sören had set snares, and his hard work had paid off. One of the wild pigs that roamed the countryside had found itself ensnared, and while boars were deadly animals, a hungry Dane was a much more significant threat.

He'd cleaned the animal and skinned it, packing it in snow and water to give the meat a hard freeze. It should keep them both for the winter. In the meantime, he had gone to get more wood, though the pile was large enough to last until next winter. While he did this, she roasted selected cuts over the fire. She supplemented that with some tubers from her dwindling collection.

He'd been on his feet for weeks now, he'd even been with her through the equinox, but as the days slowly grew longer, he became more and more restless. Still, he hadn't touched her, though she'd made little secret that his touch would be welcomed.

She would catch him looking at her. The dusky, lustful looks she'd seen other men give her when they thought she wasn't looking. The villagers and even the Lord, to a certain extent, feared her and gave her a wide berth. It was a superstition her mother had cultivated as the sole barrier of protection for a single woman alone in the woods.

This Dane, this Sören, he knew what she was. He called her a Volva; he said it meant "seer" or "wise woman." The words sounded fine but rang hollow. Everyone knew Danes were ravenous monsters who indiscriminately killed everyone they contacted. This was turning out to be as untrue as were many of her assumptions.

In the meantime, she was getting further and further frustrated with him and how he shrank from her touch. A little of the marauding, ravenous giant would be welcomed.

From a shelf in the back of the cottage, far from the heat of the flame, she pulled down a wooden bowel of rust-coloured powder. She'd sold tons of the potion to the lovelorn, awaiting the attentions of future mates who seemed immune to the age-old rituals of lovemaking.

"Spread three pinches over his food, and he will fall madly, passionately in love with you." How many times had she said that to old women, blushing maids and fat, balding men? She shook her head and replaced it on the shelf. There were two reasons not to use that powder on him. First, she didn't want him to fall into her arms because she had forced him there. She wanted to be desired, to have him hold her because he wanted to, not from some damn spell. The other reason, of course, was that it didn't work. It was a sham potion her mother made because so many asked for it, and it was easier to give them something than to try and explain why there was no such thing.

The only thing the powder did was give the users the confidence to declare themselves. They truly believed their intended was under a spell and, therefore, safe to hear their protestations of affection. Sometimes that was all that was needed.

She returned to the fire, and the occasional spit and crackle as the fat sizzled the meat and landed on the firewood. She considered the powder and thought of declaring her...affection? ...love?

All she knew was that she hadn't known how empty her life was before he was in it. The day he left to find his colony would be the worst, most lonely day of her life.

She stared into the flames and considered the real magic of the powder, and she began to plot. The more she thought it, the wider her smile became.

Carefully she used her knife to slice through a couple of threads of her bodice. It was an old dress, the other two were in better shape. One she saved for the feast day and the occasional fair.

He stayed out working on the table, gathering more wood, adding what mud and straw he could manage to scrape from the frozen ground to caulk the drafts between logs. He spent the bulk of the daylight hours outside, coming in when the sun dipped below the horizon, and the temperatures took a corresponding dive.

They ate on the newly repaired table. He had worked extra hard to get it ready for the roast. He was affable as he usually was, smiling readily and filled with good humour.

"It was good." He wiped his mouth with the back of his hand and leaned back in the chair. The wood protested at the bulk of him shifting but held. "If there was mead, now..." he grinned at the thought of it, and she rolled her eyes.

"You've been talking about mead since you woke," she teased, "So go find a honeycomb and make some. I want to try it now."

She rose and reached across the table to gather up the clay dish he'd used for his meal. She shrugged her shoulders forward slightly to loosen the bodice and bent over to retrieve the plate, letting the fabric fall as she moved.

She gave him a long look down the front of her dress. She wasn't a big woman. In fact, she could be charitably called "slender," but there was enough there to get a man's attention. Or so she thought.

At first, she thought it might be working. She could see his eyes widen and his breath catch. He almost spoke; his mouth opening and closing but once before he looked away, suddenly interested in the table leg.

"No wobble." He shoved the table back and forth, testing the integrity of the repair.

She set the plates down on the table again. "Speaking of legs," she said, thinking desperately, "I fear I might have injured myself. I twisted my leg this afternoon. Would you take a look to see if I might have done some damage?" Without waiting for him to answer, she gathered her skirts and pulled them up over her right leg, shifting her balance, so the entire leg was thrust toward him. "How does it look?"

Sören scrambled to his feet, nearly toppling her in his haste. She dropped the skirts merely so she could use her hands to find something to grab to keep from falling. In the end, she reached out and set her hand on his hip. "Did it look all right?"

Awkward, but hopefully coy enough to draw at least some kind of response.

"No. No, it's...good."

Through his pants, she could see once more the evidence of his excitement, but he was acting as though he were...afraid? As though she were dangerous. "I need to get my axe." He grabbed his furs and all but bolted through the door and into the cold night.

She nearly screamed in frustration and wished for all the world that she might join him if only to cool her own ardour before she went entirely mad after all.

CHAPTER 6

THE ICY WINDS STEADIED HIM. Even though the sea was half-frozen, the tang of salt in the air made him feel as though he was home. But the image of that leg, that long, lean, luscious leg…that sight was burned into his eyes, and he would never forget it. He would never want to forget it.

She was gorgeous, and when she acted as she had, it made his palms sweat. His heart raced every time she came near. And those casual touches would be his undoing yet.

Most days, they worked well together. If he had to be stranded on a foreign shore, there were worse places for him to be stuck. Here he was in the company of a lovely woman who laughed easily, was intelligent and strong…she was, in all aspects, perfect.

The problem was, Firtha was going to get herself killed. Twice now, someone from the village had braved the frozen ground to ask for herbs or unguents, and both times he'd had to hide, not an easy task for someone his size.

The first time it happened, there was no place for him to not be seen, and to leave someone out in the cold was unfriendly, to say the least. She'd slipped her arms through the top of her dress and held the bodice against her chest. It had worked, but Sören watched her bare back moving as she leaned over the slightly opened door.

If they had seen him, her life would have been forfeit. How could she not understand this? Every day he lingered, he put her in greater peril. He wanted to grab her, to take her, make her his. If he dropped his vigilance, what would come of her? She obviously wasn't looking after herself, not with the risks she took.

Then too…she was a Volva.

He took a great breath and felt the air chill his lungs, trying to make the chill cool other indicators of her effect on him.

She was so tiny, so wonderfully small, like all of her people. He thought he might have been able to hold her with one hand as if she would fit into his palm. That was an exaggeration, but there were parts of her that would fit perfectly. He'd already given over a considerable amount of time considering each one at night when her very nearness kept him awake. That line of thinking was dangerous too, but in a very different way.

The problem was he didn't want to have sex with her. Well, he didn't just want to have sex with her. He wanted to make love to her, hold her close, and protect her from harm. He wanted to make her his woman in every sense of the word.

And that was precisely what would cause her harm. He reached for a handful of snow and rubbed it in his face and behind his neck. He was tempted to shove some down his pants to numb the constant state of his desire. It was making him sore.

"Loki set my feet upon this path, showing me the perfect woman and then making sure I cannot have her." He ran his fingers through his beard and gave it a tug. "A Volva." He shook his head and belatedly remembered why he came out into the bitter cold.

He searched for the axe. He decided to continue the search even after he found it because the chill was finally taking his mind from other, more earthy desires.

He took a deep breath, felt as though he'd regained control of himself, and re-entered the cottage.

"GET OUT!" She screamed the words at him, a small explosion detonated near his head. It took him a moment, but he realized she'd thrown a plate at him.

"Firtha?" He stared, not entirely sure what had gotten into her.

"Sleep out in the snow!" He ducked as the second plate joined the first, shattering on the door and spreading in shards on the dirt floor.

By Odin, she was beautiful.

Deadly. But beautiful.

CHAPTER 7

FIRTHA'S FINGERS SPREAD WIDE, automatically searching for something else to throw, anything else. Of course, it was rather like throwing a flower at a boulder. He didn't even have the decency to duck when the dishes shattered next to him.

Her breath left her in a gasp as he covered the distance between them in a single stride. His large hands pinning her arms to her side.

"Let me go!"

"I will," he said, staring into her eyes. "First, tell me why ye be angry."

She stopped as cold and confused as if he had suddenly spoken another language altogether. "Why?" She searched his eyes to see if he was playing a trick on her. There was no treachery in his earnest look, no deceit. Despite her resolve not to, Firtha felt the heat of tears welling in her eyes.

"Am I so hideous? So horrible? I see yer body wanting mine, but…." She tried to shrug, but she might as well have broken free of iron bands as freed herself from his grasp.

He set her down so quickly she had to grab his arm to keep from falling. "Ye be beautiful." Again, his eyes revealed the truth of it. He believed what he was saying to her.

"Then why dinna ye desire me?" It came out as a plaintive whine, a childish scream, but the frustrations and pent-up emotions held her tongue, and she couldn't be calm, not anymore.

He stared at her. "For one thing, ye be a Volva."

Firtha held up a hand. "A what?" Her command of Danish had significantly improved since taking him in, but it was a word she hadn't heard before.

"A...seer. A healer. Someone who..."

"A witch?" there it was, the old hurt. The accusations of deviltry the priest tried to lay at her feet, the whispers that had followed her mother her entire life. She could endure being called a witch by the villagers. After all, they'd been through, the word coming from his lips wounded her to her core.

"I do not know that word." He spread his hands at his side. "In my country, a Volva is revered, sacred. To take you would be to..." he actually took a half step back and looked oddly confused. "It would be to rise myself to..." he struggled to find the right words.

"Wait." She shook her head as she realized what he was trying to say. "Are you saying that...I'm too good for you?"

He crossed his arms and stared her down. "You be a Volva. Ye should be the consort of kings."

"But that..." Firtha looked for the right word and finally decided on "madness. I am not..." She was at a loss for words. "I be just...me!"

"If they caught you harbouring me," he thrust a finger toward the door indicating the village or perhaps the Lord, "they would kill you. The snows are melting. There have been two visitors here already. Others will come. We cannot be caught. If we...if I am...distracted...I cannot protect you. I..."

Slapping his face made her arm ring up to her shoulder. He didn't move. "Listen to me. We have been in this cabin for nearly two months. In all that time, there have been two; two lovelorn women come for a dose of powder. And as far as kings go...." She nearly screamed, "I DINNA WANT KINGS!"

Slowly, it seemed to dawn on him what she was saying. The ardour had passed from her, burned off by her anger, but when he reached for her, she knew that she would lose the fight against keeping her arousal at bay. His hand wrapped behind her head, and he pulled her to him, bending down to press his lips against hers, his other hand reaching behind her back.

By every god there ever was, she wanted this. She grabbed the fur he wore around his shoulders and pulled, closing the last inch between them and pressed, pushing him away.

He broke off the kiss but held on to her, his expression a mix of heat and confusion. He breathed hard, as though he had run a race. His face was flushed, his eyes dark with desire. It was clear the burning lust hadn't been just hers to suppress. He looked half-feral, as though he held the demon in check only because she had pressed against him.

She thought a moment of the stupidity of men that she was untouchable because a witch was a horrible thing, or she was inaccessible because the Volva was too sacred. Did no one understand she was a woman? And as for being ever vigilant for her sake, that was just so much nonsense.

She slapped him again, primarily for being an idiot. Then, with a groan of her own, she threw her arms around his neck and claimed his mouth in a searing kiss, letting him know in no uncertain terms, just how much she wanted him.

CHAPTER 8

HIS MIND RESISTED EVEN as his hands roamed over the body he'd been lusting after for so long. A Volva wasn't for the likes of a man like him; that was someone revered and unique, no matter what she said. But in his hands she felt like a woman. Her body fit against his as though she'd been crafted solely for him. Her mouth was soft, full lips pressing against his with urgency and need that echoed his own.

This was no time to think. Heat and lust took over, filling every sense. He pressed a hand at the small of her back, bringing Firtha closer, fitting her curves to his body as he deepened the kiss. He was aware of his arousal pressing against the soft flesh of her belly. Did she mind? With a sigh of pleasure, her hands reached out, pulling them closer, until it seemed they must somehow occupy the same skin, so close were they.

His right hand lay on her thigh as he pulled the dress up, bundling the cloth at her hip as he tried to find the smooth flesh underneath. The dress was a nuisance, in his way. His left arm encircled her as he struggled with the fabric.

Laughing at his clumsiness, she dropped her arms from his neck and pulled the skirt up for him, allowing him to caress her thigh. It was as soft as his darkest dream imagined it to be. She moaned then and rubbed her other leg on his growing hardness, her tiny fists buried in the fur around his shoulders. She was small but surprisingly strong and pressing against him like she was as desperate to unite with him as he was.

His hand found her hip and then cupped her cheek. She ground against him, tearing at the fur and the clasp that held it at his throat. She slipped it off his shoulders and pulled up his shirt, her splayed fingers exploring his heated flesh.

Wondering at how her cheek fit perfectly in his hand, and he squeezed it, using his grasp to lift her, the other arm steadying her. She squealed in delight as he held her in the air, his fingers squeezing and playing with her as she bit his lips and reached down his pants.

He grunted as her fingers scraped across the healing injury on his hip, but he let it go, too intent on the pleasure of her.

She leaned back against his grasp and shimmied free of her dress until she stood in front of him, naked as a wood sprite, her hands trying to not cover her nudity. He caught the nervous flutter of her fingers and held her hands away from the body to allow him a good look at her.

She was breath-taking. She had the figure of a woman, rounded hips and long legs, breasts that tantalized and teased as she breathed. She caressed his chest, and he realized that he had lost his shirt some-where. She stepped forward again, her hand seeking his flesh as though she'd done so a thousand times before. Maybe in her mind, she had.

He certainly had.

Her hand wrapped around him, squeezing him and stroking. His hand lifted up her inner thigh and pressed into the warmth and tight hair that awaited his touch. She arched and moaned, his grunt soon following as her hand closed around his heated flesh and stroked him once.

He bent over, her hand popped free, but it was no matter. Right now what he needed was to taste her, to caress her with his tongue. He bowed to the right nipple and pulled it into his mouth, pulling and suckling, running his teeth gently over the hardening flesh.

She bucked and rolled against the fingers that explored her, making soft, pleasurable sounds, her head thrown back, her eyes closed in ecstasy. The heat of her body warmed his hands, her wetness awash over his fingers.

It wasn't enough. He needed more. The sweetest nectar came from the most beautiful flowers, and she was gorgeous. He grabbed her hips with both hands and fell to one knee, his face buried in between the softest thighs the gods had ever seen fit to give a woman.

She gasped a question as his tongue touched her, her eyes wide and startled for a moment, her fingers tangling in his hair. Instinctively she guided his head to the soft flesh. He dove into her eagerly.

Her legs shook, her knees began to buckle, but he held on to her tightly. She let go, letting him support her as she gripped the back of his head.

She began to flail about and moan, her legs shaking and her body twitching, and she grasped first his shoulders, and then his head, and then bent as his attentions sent waves of pleasure throughout her body. In the end, she clutched at him, held in place by the large, firm hands which held her. Her cries changed from whimpers to screams, a melodious sound calling him to duet with her. Her thighs rose and tried to wrap around him as she danced under the assault of his tongue.

AWARENESS RETURNED SLOWLY. The lights in her eyes resolved into the reflected glow of the fire. She had never done such things before. She'd never even heard that a joining between a man and woman could leave one in such a state. She thought of all those lovelorn waifs that came and went for a pinch of powder or the old men that came for other sorts of remedies. If they only knew what could be done with fingers and tongue, there would be little enough call for her powders.

Her legs were still unsteady, but she could stand independently if she held onto something solid. The Dane was the most solid thing in the cottage, and he was standing now, a pleased grin on his face. And a well-deserved one too.

Speaking of solid, there was something she'd left unfinished.

She smiled back at him and, with practised hands, freed him to her gaze. The sight of him stretched out in the bed had been appealing.

Standing there, in full command of his body and still visibly aroused, was too much to wrap her mind around.

On the other hand, it wasn't her mind she needed to wrap around that. Had he not already given her a gift this day? Did it not fall to her to give one in return?

She gripped him again, marvelling at the texture, the size, the width of it and wondering again if he was too big for what she intended when lights began dancing through the thick clouded glass of the window.

She let him go and stared, trying to determine what she was seeing, but the glass was too dark to see through well. He followed her gaze. Had it not been for the commotion outside, it would have been comical to watch his erection bobbing along a moment later.

"HO, THE HOUSE!" A man's voice called from the front. "OPEN IN THE NAME OF THE LORD!"

"What is it?" Sören reached for his pants. Firtha hadn't realized that the voice outside was speaking in Gaelic. She'd been talking Dane for so long.

"I dinna ken." She grabbed her dress and slipped it on over her head.

"More old men looking for magic?" Sören asked.

She shook her head, and his grin faded. "No." She felt a chill go through her. "Hide."

Terrified they would come in and find him there with her, she did the only thing she could. Before he could figure out what she was up to, she bolted from the house, ignoring the chill against her bare feet and the way the cold night air sliced through the thin shift she wore.

Six men, armed and armoured on horseback, awaited her. They carried torches and watched her approach with grim expressions. "Mistress Firtha," one of the men intoned with the gravity of a judge, "you are under arrest for conspiracy with the devil and for demonic practices."

"Who accuses me of such?" She crossed her arms and prayed Sören couldn't understand what was being said. There were six of them. They would kill him if he tried to stop them.

"I say." A thin, high voice called out. From the shadows, a seventh man emerged. The local priest, a favoured guest of the local Lord. "You have been selling cures, potions, and charms. Now I am told you have summoned a demon from Niflheim itself to be your lover."

"WHAT?"

"Look at her!" The priest levelled an accusing finger at her. "See the bruises on her lips? Her immodest dress. We heard your screams of ecstasy as we approached, harlot. Deny these charges, but the evidence is clear enough!"

"Take the witch." The leader of the men interrupted the whining charges of the priest.

She almost thanked him for silencing the reedy accusations. This was not something her Viking needed to hear.

"You will have time to confess your sins before you are burned at stake,"

"Burned at stake?" She repeated the phrase from shock. All humour and irritation vanished as the reality of her situation settled in on her. The cold now slipped through the warm glow of her post-orgasm and took hold of her heart.

She was so horrified, she hadn't realized she'd not spoken Gaelic.

"Mind your tongue, woman, you'll summon no demon this night to your aid...." The priest took a deep breath as though he were about to give a sermon. What he might have said was lost when the demon in question tore through the door.

CHAPTER 9

HE WAS EVERYWHERE AT ONCE.

Sören had his axe in his hand but was bare-chested against the freezing cold. He flew at the men with such force and such violence that the horses spooked and reared. Sören dodged flashing hooves as the riders tried to calm their mounts, and his empty hand flashed out to slap the steeds, creating more chaos.

One of the riders fell off of his horse, the beast ran off into the woods. The priest swore a decidedly unchristian oath as his mount disobediently tore through the dark trees with his rider hanging on for dear life.

One of the riders tried to swipe his torch along a sweeping arc to Sören, who caught the man's arm and lifted him bodily from his saddle and slammed him to the ground. Firtha heard the wind fly from the man who lay still, trying only to breathe and not much else.

Sören elbowed another horse, causing it to stumble, and the rider struggled to keep his mount steady. He was alive and unharmed, but Firtha thought it would be some time before he woke again.

Sören spun, axe at the ready, but the enemy had dispersed, finding the dark woods a safer place to be than with an enraged giant.

"What have you done?" Her words came out on a thin wail.

Sören stopped and stared. "I thought I was keeping you alive." He snarled and picked up a sword dropped by one of the riders. "Isn't that why you spoke in Danish?"

"They will come back." She didn't recognize her own voice. "In greater numbers, I might add. And they won't be retaken by surprise. They will kill us both, and they will burn my house, preferably with us in it."

Sören shoved the sword tip down into the hard frozen ground. It wavered like a reed in a storm. "Then we leave."

Firtha threw her hands in the air. "Where? Where can I go? Even if I leave these lands, my name will proceed me. There is nowhere safe when ye be called a witch."

Sören came to her, axe still in his hand. "Yes, there is. I told you, my people revere the vulva."

"Are you asking me to come with you?"

Sören shrugged and grinned. "It has to be better than burned at stake."

She reached back and set her hand on the hardwood of her hut. "This is the only place I have ever lived. It was my mothers."

"You are also your mother's," Sören reminded her, reaching for her and cupping her cheek with the palm of his hand. His voice was tender as he stroked her cheek with the meaty part of his thumb. "If ye be killed, would that save the house?"

Firtha shook her head. "The door disna work anyway." She stepped over the splintered wood and through the open doorway.

"I was in a hurry."

She shook her head. With no time to lose, she grabbed a bag she used for gathering herbs and shoved her two other dresses in the bottom. She loaded powder packets and jars of dried herbs and came to a sudden halt in the middle of the room.

"I have lived here all my life," she said to the fireplace, "and now there is almost nothing here to take from this place. I have...nothing."

"You will." Sören said with the certainty of a promise, "I will see to that."

She shouldered her bag and followed him out. When he stopped abruptly, she very nearly ran into him.

"What is it?"

Sören strode to one of the fallen men who still lay unconscious. "What is this?" He reached down and wrapped his giant fists in a dark cloth that lay mostly under the soldier. He pulled hard, sending the man rolling. Firtha wondered if the man was going to wake again or not.

"This?" He held the cloth in front of her like an accusation.

"It's the standard of the Lord's house." She traced the design. "It's supposed to be a wolf, but it looks more like a dog with mange."

He wrapped it in a fist, his eyes black with some remembered rage. "Why?"

"One of these returned to Denmark," he growled, "with word of my father. He was captured and not allowed to die in battle. I will not feast with my father in Valhalla because of the man who left this on the battlefield." He wadded it up and shoved it at her. "Keep this in your bag. I must show it to my brothers."

"And then?"

"And then we take this matter to the door of this Lord of yers." Sören made the answer an oath, and Firtha shuddered. He tore the cloak from the soldier and draped it around her shoulders. "Come, it will be daylight soon. The day will warm."

She huddled into the cape, doubting his definition of "warm," and followed him into the lightening woods.

He was silent as he walked. Firtha thought he was brooding on the standard he'd pulled from the soldier. By the afternoon, he was talkative again, and if the day wasn't hot, the walking helped a great deal. She threw off the cloak at one point to cool off as they walked along the coast.

As night chilled the air, they wandered further in from the coast where a fire would not be so easily seen. She gathered all the fallen wood she could find while he built a credible lean-to and used pine branches to line it and keep the winds off.

He started a fire close enough to the structure to get heat from the fire and spread out his fur to use over them both. Though Firtha knew that it would barely cover him, he wanted to be sure that she was warm that night. The cloak acted as a ground cloth, keeping their body heat from leaching into the ground.

She sidled close to him, trying to keep the furs on them both. He opened his arm, and she snuggled in beside him, remembering the earlier passion. With her head on his chest she could call to mind the way he had introduced her to passion. Even now as he stroked her back, almost idly, she felt the stirring between her loins. There was still unfinished business between them. She watched the stars slowly spin overhead and wondered how to express to him everything in her heart. She reached over and lay her arm across his chest.

His hand traced down her back and made circles on her lower back. She grinned and slipped her hand into his pants again, searching for his swollen flesh. He rolled over onto his elbow and lifted her dress, covering her with the fur. "Ye be sure?" he asked against her mouth as they kissed.

"Aye." It had been a tiring day to be sure, but she could think of no better way to end it.

She freed him from his pants, and he lay over her, a mountain of muscle. His mouth on hers was more tender than the night before but every bit as passionate.

She spread her legs, her body already arching toward him as she welcomed him there. It felt natural to be guiding him in through her folds. He was large, but he entered her slowly until he filled her completely. To her delight, he fit most satisfactorily. He held himself there until he was sure she was accommodating his girth and then began to move inside her. He pulled out slowly and waited, and pushed back in, filling her until she thought she must burst.

The speed was agonizing. She needed more. Firtha lifted her hips to meet his thrusts, and he took the hint. He sped up his thrusts, moving faster, harder. He thrust deeper into her and alternated his strokes, driving her mad and pausing when she got too close to sliding over the edge they had discovered together earlier in the day. It was maddening and intense, perfect in every way.

He drove harder, his breathing faster and shallow; she clawed his hips, urgent to feel him ever closer, to draw him even deeper. She wrapped her legs around him until they ached. The ground, so hard beneath her back was a discomfort to be ignored. It was better to be pinned to the ground than to lose so much as a moment of this passion.

Eventually, she heard him gasp and felt his tremors as his release took him. To her delight, the feel of him throbbing within her triggered her own release. Firtha spasmed around him, her orgasm pulling his own. She shuddered despite the heat of the fire and the warmth of his body on hers.

He rolled onto his back, pulling her along, so she lay on him. A much better place to rest It could even be argued he was by far more comfortable than the bed had ever been.

Firtha smiled as she drifted off to sleep.

She was home.

CHAPTER 10

THIS TIME it wasn't only six men that came for them. Nearly two dozen armed men riding warhorses, trained not to spook, bore down on the crude shelter Sören had built for them the night before.

The same captain that Sören humiliated was in charge and had something to prove to his Lord. He wasn't there to arrest; he was there to end the threat of the Viking and witch.

The company rode over the small structure, smashing through the fire's dying embers and trampling the cloak covering the two lovers. There was no resistance. There was no time for them to get away. The witch and her lover were well trampled while they slept.

The captain drew his sword to pull the cloak free of the mangled bodies. Still, instead of two crushed corpses, he found nothing more than fir branches stuffed under the cloak to make it look as though there were two people asleep.

He screamed in frustration and ordered his men to branch out and find them, to bring them to him alive if possible.

As the men split and began searching the woods, a single boat that had slipped its mooring floated without direction on the tide. It spun in slow, lazy circles as it wandered down the coastline, a local's loss under the morning sun.

Firtha lay on her Viking again, fighting sleep and trusting in the uncanny navigation of a Norseman as the boat seemed to find its own way. She heard the distant screams of rage and the shouted orders of the captain and felt the deep chuckle in her lover's chest as he laughed at the foolish men who thought they could stop them.

Nothing could stop them, not anymore.

Firtha was sore, but it was a delicious kind of soreness. The kind you welcomed after a short respite. He was large, but he was patient, and she snuggled against him in the bottom of the stolen boat, bobbing in the waters off the coast as it slowly carried them to her future.

When she dared to peek over the side of the craft, but she could see nothing but the rocky coastline and the stunted trees of Scotland. The hate and fear were gone, hidden behind the darkness of the wood.

She smiled down at her Viking. "I think 'tis safe to sit up."

"Safe," he agreed, a savage smile on his face. "but not nearly so... interesting."

He shifted the fur and somehow got his hand under her dress.

She had to agree, especially when her wandering hand found flesh more interesting than her own to touch. He responded to her clever fingers and their explorations of his body with a soft groan and a curse as his reaction nearly upset the boat.

Later, when they had dressed and sat up, he grabbed the oar and aimed them for shore. Firtha saw a great building, a long structure made of timber and thatch surrounded by smaller homes.

"The Greathouse," Sören crowed as though she should know what the word meant.

A group of warriors stood on the shore, hands on the hilts of their swords, waiting for them to make landfall.

"Abjörn!" Sören screamed and waved his arms wildly.

"Sören?" One of the men began laughing and waded into the water as fast as possible, disregarding the cold. He reached the boat in moments, just about tackling his brother as he and Sören embraced. They slapped each other's backs and grinned. It was like seeing double.

"My brother!" Sören crowed, though the descriptor was unnecessary. He pointed to Firtha. "This is my brother Abjörn. This is Firtha. She is a Volva." He paused a moment and shot her bright smile, "and my wife."

Wife?

Abjörn then gave her a wet embrace that nearly capsized the boat. "WELCOME," he bellowed, and then he clapped his brother's arm. "We thought you died! Only my little brother could die and come back to life with a beautiful bride. And a Volva at that!" He grabbed the boat and dragged them back to shore, chattering away about his little brother and how the other brothers grieved for him.

Wife.

Firtha found herself smiling bigger and brighter than she ever remembered having done. She rather liked the word but couldn't help but think it might have been nice to have at least had a ceremony of some kind.

I have a Viking.

Or maybe it wasn't necessary after all.

EPILOGUE

ABJÖRN and his brothers gathered in the hut. Sören's new wife was adapting well. She already had a long line of women and men at her doorstep wanting powders and cures.

But Sören had insisted that the brothers meet alone. He carried the bag he had when she'd arrived.

They had celebrated his safe return with a feast and then his marriage with another. As long as the mead held out, they would be welcoming the new Volva to their colony, but today, Sören's face held no joy.

"Do you remember the cloth that Olaf brought to us and what was said?"

"I do." Erik brought a scrap of cloth from his pouch. He dropped it on the table. It was the stylized head of a wolf. "Olaf said it was taken from a soldier who took father when he was betrayed. He said they all wore it."

Sören reached into the bag and unfurled a large black cloth. The design matched.

"The king in these lands gave us this land as Danegeld. The local Lord seems to be unhappy with the arrangement."

"You think he killed our father?" Ryker grabbed the scrap and compared them.

"Trussed up like a pig for slaughter." Sören nodded. "Without honour, without courage. He betrayed our father and sent him to Niflheim."

"Then we kill him." Abjörn nodded slowly. "He has broken the truce and his king's word."

They will think we have broken the truce," Erik said softly, his voice uncertain.

"Then we raise the Danegeld," Abjörn said with a lopsided grin, "until they can no longer pay it."

"Allowing us to raid and plunder these shores as we wish," Erik said with satisfaction.

THE END

ABJÖRN

LURED BY AN ENGLISH ROSE

PROLOGUE

ABJÖRN STILL BLAMED himself for the shipwreck that almost killed them all and forced them to winter in this strange place. However, he could finally sleep, knowing his brother Sören was alive. He hated being separated for those winter months but seeing his brother happy with his new bride warmed his heart. Abjörn, and the rest of the Jürgensen brothers, couldn't remember a time when Sören was so happy. The love of a good woman would do that.

While they celebrated their brother's return, the Jürgensen brothers' hearts were heavy with the news he brought with him. The man who killed their father called these lands his home. Abjörn and his brothers were smart and often underestimated, as most Danes were. Thought to be all brawn and no brains. Abjörn proved such thinking wrong by coming up with the idea to raise the Danegeld. Once it reached untenable levels, they knew it wouldn't be long before the Lord came looking for them. Let the Lord start the fight, not them. Why waste your energy chasing the mouse when you can lure it in with cheese?

Abjörn examined the map that Firtha had drawn up. Abjörn admired her penmanship; the lines detailed the shortcut through the valley and past the border. She knew these strange lands like the back of her hand and didn't hesitate to describe the dwelling of the English Lord near the border.

Abjörn and Ryker travelled over the hill and down through the valley. Each step took them closer to avenging their father's death. The map guided them through the thickest of trees, wide enough to hide even them. The hills over the Lord's castle were steep enough to tire out most men. But they were not most men. They were Vikings, some of their people's biggest and strongest examples.

Abjörn and Ryker circled the woods surrounding the Lord's castle hunting for the perfect vantage point. Finally, they found it behind moss-covered boulders hidden by the thicket of trees atop the hill.

"We should set up camp at the bottom of the valley. Smoke from our fire will go unnoticed from there," Ryker suggested. Abjörn nodded, keeping his eyes on the castle entrance guarded by men wearing the cape with the wolf sigil, confirming they had found the right place.

"It won't be long now, brother; we raised the Danegeld. He has to take notice," Abjörn said, stroking the handle of his axe with his thumb. He itched for battle.

"How long do you think we should stay?" Ryker asked, making himself comfortable against a nearby tree, the wood protesting against his giant size.

"A man like him will not wait to attack," Abjörn said, staring intently at the castle.

Abjörn was right. Three nights of stalking their prey paid off. "Look," Abjörn said, slapping his brother's shoulder with the back of his strong hand. The armed guard had doubled from two men at the door to four. A small army of soldiers guarded the castle gate as a small dark wagon was pulled by a pair of black English Great horses. Abjörn liked horses and thought how nice it would be to add the heavy draft animals to the collection back at the settlement. The guards waiting outside followed as the wagon moved out of the castle grounds, guarding it closely.

"You see that?" Abjörn asked Ryker, pointing to the seat next to the driver.

Huddled next to the driver sat a small figure hidden by a long black hooded cloak; the back of the wagon was packed with three small wooden trunks tied securely with rope and chains. They followed the wagon as it slowly worked its way west up the road.

"Travelling trunks? Who do you think is under that cloak?" Ryker asked as they moved between the trees, keeping the wagon in clear sight.

"I don't know but given the size of the force that surrounds it, whoever it is must be of some importance," Abjörn replied as his mind tried to make sense of the situation.

The settlement was back to the east. Where was the wagon going with such a heavy guard? Was the Lord sending the cavalry before coming for Abjörn and his brothers? What treasure was the Lord removing that required three trunks under such heavy guard?

"Ryker, head back to the settlement, inform the others of what we have witnessed. Something is not right. We must prepare," Abjörn said, pulling his furs tighter around his neck. "I will follow and find out what manner of treasure our friend the Lord intends to hide. Then we attack. Revenge is so close, brother," Abjörn said, receiving a stern agreeable nod from Ryker before he swiftly descended the hill and headed home.

CHAPTER 1

SIMA WAS FURIOUS. Her father was treating her like a prisoner. It made her sick. This particular wagon was usually used for errands by the servants, transporting hay to the stables or grain from the markets. To ride in such a thing was a disgrace. The seat creaked underneath her as the wheels struggled against the mask left from winter. The snow had stopped, but the air was still bitterly cold, causing her breath to freeze on the air. She struggled with her bonds as the rope tore her skin.

Her mind flashed back to the fight with her father before he carted her off. "It's for your protection, you are going, and that's final," he had said to her.

Sima was known amongst the court for having what some deemed as a temper, but she never saw it that way. On the contrary, she prided herself in being different from all the other women at court. While most of the court ladies had a collection of handmaids to tend to their every need, Sima refused to be coddled. She was capable of bathing and dressing all by herself, "I am not a babe fresh off the breast," she had insisted.

Sima never thought of herself as an angry woman; just different. She was independent, strong-minded, and wasn't afraid to act in ways that most would think unladylike, such as when faced with an overzealous gentleman.

"Protection from what, father?" she had asked.

"Nothing a lady should concern herself with," was her father's reply.

"When you try and remove me from my home, it is my concern," she argued.

A war is on the horizon with the Vikings. That is all you need to know. Now pack your things. It has already been arranged you leave at once!" he bellowed, his voice bouncing off the strong stone walls.

"Vikings? Are they not men? I am not afraid of men, be it a Viking, a King's guardsman, or a Celt. I am more than capable of defending myself. I am not one of those fragile little things you are so fond of. Ask your guards. How is the captain's nose, by the way?" she said smugly.

Earlier that month, when the captain of her father's guard had gotten overly friendly, she'd kicked him in the groin and broke two ribs and his nose.

Her father looked back at her, full of amusement, "Ask him yourself," he told her. And before she could argue any further, two guards, one being the captain, had grabbed her and bound her hands. She was flung over a shoulder, kicking and screaming down to the wagon.

The wagon tipped slightly as the wheel hit a hole in the road, bringing Sima back into reality. She wasn't one to cry, but as the wagon drew closer and closer to the convent, she felt more inclined to weep. More in frustration and anger than sadness. *It's ok, father, I will show you precisely what I'm capable of,* she thought to herself, mentally mapping the landscape for her journey back home once she escaped.

The convent looked as cold and miserable as Sima imagined it would. But, to her surprise, as they drew closer, it was plain to see the structure was bigger and more well-built than she thought. Escaping was going to be trickier than she thought. The wagon stopped outside the gates waiting for someone to open them before travelling down the long dark road to the convent entrance. *Why is this place guarded like a fortress?* Sima asked herself as she scanned her surroundings, looking for gaps in walls and fences for when she made her escape.

Her father's guards presented her to the two nuns waiting by the big oak door. "There is no need for the bonds. Remove them, please," the oldest nun said sweetly.

Finally, Sima thought to herself, rubbing her reddened wrists.

The two nuns gently guided her into the cold convent. Sima grimaced as the smell of musk and damp earth filled her lungs. The ground inside was wet, almost like it had been raining. The walls were bare except for a slimy residue coating them from the many leaks in the roof. Sima wrapped her arms around herself, feeling the cold air nip at her skin and making her nipples harden, creating two little mountains against her bodice.

"After we show you to your room, you can change. We dress simpler here," the old nun said, eyeing her charge's rather inadequate dress.

Sima ignored the woman. Instead, she memorised the maze of corridors and chambers. She didn't intend on staying the night.

Sima looked around the room at the top of the stairs. The nuns told her that her father had requested the best room. The room was bare except for a cot in the corner with a small itchy woollen blanket. There was a table and chair on the other side of the room, under a small window. The air hissed through the cracked wooden shutters. These shutters were barely clinging to life. Sima knew if she tried to open them, they would fall out the window entirely and plummet to the ground below. Draped over the chair was a long plain dress, once white, but had been washed so many times that it had taken on a pale shade of brown. Sima picked it up to look at it, and the fabric was just as scratchy as the blanket.

The conditions her father expected her to live in only fuelled the fire within her. "For my protection," she huffed, pacing the room. "Who is going to protect me from this?" she raged under her breath. She had not removed her cloak since she arrived. She huddled in it now, thinking it would barely save her from the almost freezing temperatures of the convent. It would suffice to keep her warm when she left.

She waited until the sun was starting to descend over the hills. The convent was poorly lit. She planned to use that to her advantage. She didn't worry about her belongings. She would have her father fetch them when she arrived back home. She longed to see the look on his face when his plan to be rid of her failed. She had her escape all worked out. If she were found wandering outside her room past dark, she would tell the nuns she was trying to familiarise herself with her new home.

When she opened the door, she stepped back momentarily, shaken to see a man's form towering over her. He was tall and built like a mountain. His dark hair fell in a controlled, chaotic mess over his head and moulded beautifully into his thick dark beard. His eyes seemed to sparkle when they travelled down her body, lingering over her chest.

Oh my, what a sight for sore eyes, she thought, biting her bottom lip as she often did when she was faced with an attractive man. She was partial to a man with facial hair. To Sima, it was a sign of unbridled masculinity. She wondered how it would feel to run her fingers through his coarse hair and feel it brushing against her skin.

"Has my father sent you to guard my door?" she asked in a breathy whisper.

Wordlessly, he shook his head slowly while his eyes settled on her chest, which was rising and falling rapidly.

"Good. Now I order you to get me out of this place and take me back to my home. I must speak with that brute who thinks he controls me. I must speak with my father immediately."

CHAPTER 2

HE COULDN'T BELIEVE his luck. Not only had he found the Lord's most prized treasure, but she also wasn't even afraid of him. Abjörn wasn't a dense man. He could tell that she found him just as attractive as he did her. And with his mission in mind, he planned on using that to his advantage.

She stood tall and slender. The cloak wrapped around her shoulders barely covered her beautiful breasts contained in her blue velvet bodice. He revelled in how they rose and fell as her breathing quickened, and he could feel his attraction fighting to be released from his clothing. For a moment, he forgot why he was there. Her beauty mesmerised him. Abjörn had never seen a woman so beautiful.

No wonder the Lord tried to hide her from the world. She truly is a treasure of high value, he thought to himself.

When she asked him a question, he shook his head, trying to buy himself time while he thought. She was not fazed by his size or stature, which impressed him. Abjörn was the biggest and tallest of his brothers. A woman who was not afraid of a Viking warrior like him was something to behold.

"If you help me, I shall reward you with a kiss," she said, blinking seductively at him.

By all the gods, she was trying to seduce him. What a ridiculous notion! Abjörn would not be distracted from his mission of getting revenge on the Lord…but then, what sweeter revenge was there than to deflower the Lord's precious daughter.

He ducked under the door frame standing at his full height in front of her causing her to step back and arch her neck to look up at him. Her cloak fell off her shoulders, fully exposing her bosom to his enjoyment.

Abjörn grabbed her gently by the shoulders and spun her around, trapping her between him and the wall. Taking a fist full of her hair in one hand, he gently pulled back, exposing her neck to him, causing her to pant a little. Looking into her eyes, he could see that she wanted it too. He brought his lips down to hers, pushing his tongue into her mouth, allowing it to explore her. He was surprised to feel her tongue massage his in return. She tasted so sweet. Abjörn allowed his other hand to pull up her skirt and explore her thigh. He felt the warmth between her legs and permitted himself to enjoy the slick warmth with his fingers.

He pulled away and grazed her neck with his teeth before his lips trailed over her breasts. When she let out a moan of enjoyment, he stepped back, gazing at her, knowing she too felt the attraction between them.

"Come," he said, his voice low. Grabbing her wrist, he dragged her behind him down the stairs and through the maze of corridors.

Revenge has never been so easy…or enjoyable, he thought to himself as she struggled to keep up with his long strides.

"Unhand me," she whispered angrily.

Abjörn knew she wouldn't protest too much. She wanted out of this place. "Stop…be quiet," he whispered, stopping at the corner of the last corridor before the entrance. He listened to the echoes bouncing off the walls; the sounds carried on the wind.

Revenge without breaking a sweat; this certainly is a first. How will the Lord react when he finds out I have tasted his unspoilt flower. He licked his lips, still tasting her on his tongue.

CHAPTER 3

SIMA WAS NOT in the mood for this nonsense. The big oaf hadn't even spoken a word to her before eyeing her like a hungry wolf would eye a lamb. She offered the kiss but never expected to be taken in the way he did. Even if she had enjoyed his touch and the roughness of his beard on her skin, she was furious that he presumed he could just take what he wanted. Did he not know who she was? She had broken noses for less. While she couldn't deny how her body had responded to him and she couldn't deny that she found him handsome, the nerve of him only added to the anger that had been brewing deep within her all day long.

She could have forgiven him if he would have finished what he started. Getting her all hot and bothered, only to stop and drag her away. Annoying to say the least. He hadn't even offered his name. Between her father having her bound and carted away and this stranger bruising her wrists as he pulled her forcefully through the convent, she had reached her tolerance for being mistreated for the day.

At this point, Sima didn't know what frustrated her more. The big oaf dragged her with no regard for her feelings or protests, or the feeling that his touch had roused between her thighs. The feeling that craved release.

He stopped again as the corridor widened before the big oak door that she had entered upon her arrival. He listened for anyone approaching. Sima took this as her opportunity for freedom and to release some of her pent-up frustrations. She pulled her arm from his grasp, and as he turned to take hold of her once more, she brought her knee to his groin. With lust still flowing like a river in her veins, she tried to ignore the hard, thick length she felt when her knee connected with his groin. There was a moment of curiosity, at its size and taste, but she pushed the thoughts to the back of her mind and ran.

She had no doubt that she could find her way home from the convent, but the door was heavier than she thought. She pulled at the big round mental handle with all her might, but it only moved a morsel. Not nearly enough for her to squeeze through before her newfound captor recovered and came looking for her.

CHAPTER 4

ABJÖRN GROANED WITH ANGER. The sound rumbled through the halls like the growl of a bear. Whatever attraction he felt for this woman moments ago had now vanished. She had seen to that. He was still carrying the effects of their encounter in her room when her knee made contact. While her guts and strength impressed him, they also angered him. She was strong, but not enough to cause any real pain or damage. His groin ached slightly, and it took a moment or two before he could stand up straight without pain shooting through his stomach. But in a few short strides – short to a man his size anyway - he had caught up to her at the door.

Her eyes widened as he approached, as frantically she squeezed her slender frame through the crack in the door. Flinging it open, no longer caring if he was caught, he ran after her up the road to the front gate. He grabbed her around the waist and flung her over his shoulder like a bag of grain.

"Unhand me, you brute! Wait until my father hears about this," she shrieked, kicking her legs out and slamming her fists into his back. Her temper tantrum amused Abjörn. She was trying to hurt him, but all he felt was a tickle.

Abjörn scanned his surroundings as he headed for a small break in the wall where the bricks had crumbled. The woods would make a good cover. Her backside perched nicely in his line of sight; he was pleasantly distracted by how it bounced in time with his strides. So taken was he by the sight that he nearly tripped over a fallen tree.

Frustrated that he had allowed himself to be distracted, he stormed onward. Unfortunately, she continued to yell. If she didn't quiet, she would alert the guards still sheltered in the convent. While Abjörn was confident that he could fight off all of them on his own, he didn't want to have to. He needed her to be quiet.

She let off a surprised gasp as his hand connected with her backside. "Hush, woman!" he said, striding up the hill to where he had left his horse.

"Woman? Do you not know to whom you speak?" she shrieked.

"I do not care," he replied.

His horse was hidden amongst the trees at the top of the hill. It was a magnificent black beast, as tall and as muscular as Abjörn, with large white patches of hair hanging over its solid, broad hooves. Whinnying as they approached and tapping its front foot. Abjörn smiled. "There you are, old friend," he said, stroking the horse's long white mane.

Abjörn grabbed Sima and placed her on the front of his horse before quickly mounting behind her. Wrapping his arms around her so she wouldn't jump or fall, he gripped the reins and commanded his horse to move forward.

The movement of their bodies in time with the horse caused them to grind up against each other. The wind blew in their faces, which drifted her floral fragrance with it. Abjörn found the smell intoxicating. A memory of the scent as he ran his lips over her neck flashed in his mind. He tried to fight it, but his arousal grew, causing him to shift uncomfortably in the saddle.

He didn't want her to know the effect she had on him. Abjörn didn't want to give her that power. A woman who knows her impact on a man is a dangerous thing. A woman with that power could bring a man like Abjörn to his knees.

CHAPTER 5

SIMA GAVE UP STRUGGLING. He had wrapped his large, muscular arms tightly around her. There was no way she could escape. Adrenaline added to her already aroused state. The combination of friction from the saddle and the strong arms holding her in place was almost too much for her. She allowed herself to sink back into his arms. She felt oddly comforted in his embrace. The few men who had shared her bed had never left her feeling as crazed as she did at that moment.

Her mind flashed back to their encounter earlier. In truth, she liked how forceful, yet tender he was with her. The way he gripped her hair, claiming her. She could feel herself growing damp from the memory.

"As I am your prisoner, may I at least know your name?" she asked.

"Abjörn," he replied, and she felt a thrill run through her as his breath brushed against her ear.

Abjörn, she repeated in her mind. Even his name sounded solid and mysterious. She offered her name in response. "I am Sima."

She didn't know all of her father's men, primarily due to his ever-changing roster – her father found it hard to trust even the men he chose to guard his family. Still, she knew some of the names of the men who had been in her father's staff the longest. Ailwin, Colin, Halyas, but the name Abjörn was one she had never come across before.

That's a Viking name, she realised belatedly, alarm running through her. Her father had warned her about an impending war; she never expected to be caught in the middle of it. She also never expected to be fantasising about a Viking taking her hard in the woods. "You are not one of my father's men," she said out loud.

"No, I am not," he replied, and she sensed anger in his tone.

"Viking?" she asked, already knowing the answer.

A grunt of agreement was Abjörn's only reply.

This could be an opportunity for Sima to prove to her father how valuable she is and make him see what a mistake it was to underestimate her and banish her to that convent. *If I get information from him, I could inform father before this war escalates,* she thought.

"You speak my language so elegantly," she said, attempting flattery.

"I speak Gaelic and four other languages," he replied.

"What do you want from me?" she asked, gently leaning back further into his embrace. She could feel his hard flesh pushing against her back. Lust once again seeped through her. She had heard of the lovemaking skills of Viking men but thought it all court gossip, until she felt his tool not once, but twice, in less than an hour.

"Nothing from you," he replied dryly. At that moment, she had all the answers she needed. This wasn't about her. This was about her father.

Sima suddenly realised something. For the first time in her life, she was afraid of a man. She was scared of this Viking Abjörn. "Do you intend to hurt my father?" she asked meekly.

"Your father has committed crimes he needs to answer for."

"You haven't answered my question."

"No, I do not intend to hurt him," he replied, allowing Sima enough room to breathe. "I intend to kill him." He finally said, and Sima felt a cold chill down her spine.

"I am the daughter to Lord Beecham," she started.

"I know who you are," he interjected.

"What could I give you that would allow you to spare my family?"

"You have nothing I want," he said coolly.

"I have gold and silver," she continued, but he didn't respond. She thought it best to argue her cause with the only real power women had. She offered herself.

She pushed her firm buttocks further back into him and ground her hips. She felt him growing at her touch. He shifted behind her, trying to move out of her reach. That's when she knew she had him in the palm of her hand.

"I have something more valuable," she purred, taking one of his large rough, calloused hands and tucking it inside her bodice. She sucked in a sharp breath as his fingers brushed against her nipples, which already stood at attention, begging to be touched.

"You can have me, do anything you want with me," she purred again, letting her head rest on his chest." You could take me right here in these woods," she continued removing his hand and encouraging it to slide under her skirt, pulling it closer and closer to the sweet spot between her legs that throbbed, wanting to be touched. "Spare my family, and I will be yours."

He pulled on the reins hard, stopping the horse so abruptly that she almost fell off headfirst. He dismounted, grabbed her hips, and pulled her from the horse. He dragged her to a nearby tree, slamming her back hard into it before putting his strong hands on her shoulders. "You can try and seduce me, but his blood runs in your veins. I do not want sex with you; I do not want anything from you," he growled.

"You can deny it all you want, but what happened in the convent and your arousal stabbing me in the back betrays you," she said.

Abjörn stared at her, his eyes burning deep into hers. His brow furrowed, and his grip tightened on her shoulders, causing her to wince. "My father will not dine with us in Vallhalla because of your father. Your father sentenced him to Hel. My father was a gentle man, a fearsome warrior who fought for peace and justice. A light in the dark and your father left him to die without honour."

Sima winced, feeling her heart ache for him. His Viking's face raged with anger, but his eyes cried with sorrow.

"How do you know it was my father? There are many Lords in this land. It could have been any of them," Sima insisted, still wanting to do what she could to save her family. She didn't want to believe what this man said was true. She might have been angry with her father for sending her to the convent, but he was a good man. Wasn't he?

"The King gave my people land. And when my father met with yours to discuss Danegeld, a peaceful meeting, your father betrayed him. The soldier who killed him wore your father's sigil. A betrayal like this cannot go unpunished." He told her.

I remember that meeting, I asked to go with him, but he said Vikings are savages and wouldn't take me, Sima thought, trying not to let her face betray her. "I'm sorry, but I, my family, are not my father. I have a mother and sisters and a brother. Why should they suffer for the sins of the father?" she begged.

Sima pushed herself free of his grip but stayed where she was, running her hand over his chest and down to his crotch. "I know you want me. Why deny it? I'm giving myself to you," she whispered seductively in his ear. She reached for his belt where she saw the glint of a blade, but he saw through her. He grabbed her wrist and spun her around, pulling her back into him. "Nice try," he chuckled, pulling a rope from his belt and binding her again.

Sima noticed how, when binding her, he could not seem to help how his hands explored her body.

CHAPTER 6

ABJÖRN DIDN'T BELIEVE his own words, but he hoped she did. Of course, he wanted her. The thought of taking her right there against the tree gave him feelings he struggled to control.

She was the most beautiful woman he had ever seen. Feeling her grind against him in the saddle had been torture. He knew she had felt his arousal. Tasting her, however briefly, had been a mistake. Since then, his blood burned with lust. He wanted to rip her bodice off and take her large breasts into his mouth.

When she had guided his hand under her skirt, he felt how wet she had become. She may have been offering herself as a ploy to save her family, but there was also some truth there. She wanted him too, which just made him want her all the more.

The thought of taking her just because she offered wasn't satisfying enough. Abjörn wanted her to want him, to feel her long legs wrapped around his waist, to feel his shaft stretch her and have her grip him tightly in response. He wanted to hear her moan with pleasure in his ear, knowing he was the cause. He wanted to listen to her scream his name.

She fought against him, but Abjörn was too strong for her. He was impressed with her determination and the fact that she was not afraid of him. She was a strong woman in more ways than one. Her mind was just as strong as her will. It just made her all the more appealing to Abjörn.

She would make a fine Viking bride, he thought. His hands ran over her stomach as she twisted in his grasp. To come home from battle to see her waiting with open arms, caring for the children, and tending to the farm. The thought startled him. How had she managed to distract him from his mission?

He was here to get revenge on Lord Beecham. He was here to avenge his father and gain forgiveness for causing the shipwreck that stranded them here. His mind raced while in her presence; he couldn't keep focused on his cause. They had covered enough distance from the convent. Maybe another kiss would settle the lust in him enough for now.

Horses and footsteps in the distance brought his mind back to attention. A feeling of disappointment twisted in his gut. He wished he had more time alone with Sima. He was curious to see if the both of them would give in to their primal urges.

"My brothers approach," he said, scooping her up in his arms and then flinging her atop of the horse. Taking the reins, he walked towards the rumbling of footsteps. "Brothers," he yelled, a smile spanning his face.

"Who is there?" asked a voice Abjörn had never heard before. Squinting his eyes to try and focus the figures through the trees, he and Sima came to the same conclusion at once.

"It's my father's men; they must have discovered I had fled," she said, looking down from the horse, her eyes filled with worry. Odd. She had shown she was not afraid of him, so why should she be scared now?

"Run, Abjörn; you are outnumbered," she said, and he realised she cared for him. It was a thought worth exploring later. Little did she know even ten of her father's men were no match for him and the two axes tucked into his belt.

Five men on horseback came through the clearing. Each had a broadsword strapped to their hip. Helms covered their heads and descended their noses. The look on their faces told Abjörn they had not expected to find a Viking. No one said a word when they realised whom he had with him. For a moment, the only sounds were the wind rustling the leaves in the trees and the heavy breathing of their horses.

"Unhand, Lady Beecham," bellowed one of the guards.

"You want her, come claim her!" He grinned, pulling an axe from his right hip.

The men chuckled amongst themselves. By their way of thinking, the Viking was outnumbered. "Lady Beecham, I'll protect you from this savage beast," said the captain as he dismounted his horse. Abjörn looked up at Sima, who only rolled her eyes. Abjörn laughed to himself. He was about to humiliate her father's men and looked forward to the task.

The captain drew his sword and swung at Abjörn, who ducked and sidestepped quickly. They danced their dance for a minute or two as Abjörn let the captain tire himself out. Occasionally looking up to Sima, whom he could tell was finding the humiliation of her father's guard captain amusing.

"Hit him already!"

"Come on, captain!" came the cheers from his men.

The captain panted heavily and struggled to raise his sword as his muscles surely ached from failed attacks on Abjörn.

"Enough of this," Abjörn said, sending his axe through the air as the captain raised his sword above his head. The axe embedded itself in the captain's chest. The captain fell to the ground with a thud. Abjörn used his boot to roll the body over and pulled the axe from his chest.

"Who's next?" he asked, pulling the axe from his left hip, standing tall, ready to fight.

CHAPTER 7

THE SOLDIERS SAT on their horses, eyeing each other nervously.

They should be nervous; my Viking is fierce, Sima thought to herself. In her mind, she had already claimed him as her own.

She was more aware now of the effect she had over him because the ropes binding her were not as tight as she expected. She kept a close eye on her Viking standing ready to attack; masculinity, bravery, and ruggedness in one handsome package. In the meantime, she twisted and wriggled, trying to free herself.

She heard a branch crack and looked to the trees behind her father's soldiers, who had since decided to be brave and dismount, circling Abjörn. Men wearing similar clothing and furs carrying axes and daggers crept closer. Each one was almost as big and tall as Abjörn. *These must be his brothers,* she thought. They burst through the trees, spooking the horses who bolted as the Vikings' roars still echoed on the winds.

"Steady boy," Sima said, gripping the saddle, trying to stop her horse from getting riled up and tossing off its back.

The animal would not be calmed. The horse bucked and whinnied as Sima struggled to control the panicked beast as chaos erupted around them.

Sima couldn't help but notice how Abjörn had worked his way

between her and her father's guards. She admired how he had decided to act as her shield.

He was magnificent in battle. Abjörn moved so fluidly for a man of his size and build. To move more freely, he had removed the furs over his shoulders. Sima knew he was a muscular man from how he had carried her. She'd had those sculpted arms wrapped tightly around her on that very horse. But seeing his muscles bulge around his shoulders and neck as he fought had Sima wanting to run her hands all over him.

Her father's men were no match for these mountains of men. Even with their broadswords, the skills of the Vikings were unmatched. Sima had never been a woman with much interest in the inner workings of battle, but as she sat astride the horse and watched, she found it oddly fascinating.

The horse, she thought, snapping back into reality. She enjoyed watching the battle, but she needed to go home. She finally wriggled free and pulled the rope off, tossing it on the dirt at Abjörn's feet.

"Goodbye, Abjörn," she said with a grin. He glanced behind; his eyes widened as he saw she had freed herself.

"No!" he yelled, reaching for the reins, but she turned the horse, kicking its ribs, sending the beast running into the forest, taking her back towards her home.

The sound of swords and axes clashing, and angry grunts diminished as she galloped further away from the fight. While she was filled with joy as home drew closer, her loins ached at the thought of never feeling her Viking between her legs.

CHAPTER 8

THE GROUND WAS SOAKED in the blood of Lord Beecham's men. The battle continued longer than needed. Abjörn could have taken them alone and with ease. However, after knowing these soldiers' involvement in their father's demise, the brothers wanted to savour the moment.

Sören pulled the cloak from one of the soldiers and used it to clean the blade of his axe. "These men are no match for father. It makes me wonder what happened that day," Sören said, picking up a discarded broadsword and testing its weight.

"We will find out shortly," Abjörn replied, staring off in the direction the woman he longed for had galloped, taking his horse and his sanity along with her. Ryker clapped him hard around the back "you're losing your touch in your old age. I have never known you to lose a woman and a horse. In the same day, no less," he laughed, erupting a chorus of laughter from the rest of his brothers. "I will get her back," he whispered to the wind.

"She was the hooded figure in the wagon. Her name is Sima Beecham," Abjörn said, turning to pick up his furs and wrap them back over his shoulder.

"The Lord's woman?" Ryder asked.

"Better, his eldest daughter," Abjörn replied.

"She will be heading back to the Lord's castle, no doubt to warn her father and gather more forces," Erik said as he searched the bodies of the dead soldiers for gold and anything else of value.

The plan was to allow the Lord to attack. First, Abjörn worried they had started the war prematurely; they needed more means before they could attack Beecham's castle. Once Sima made it back and informed her father of the day's events, his men would undoubtedly come looking for the Jürgensen brothers.

"Brothers, it's time to for raiding," Dittmer said; he had ventured off and brought back one of the soldier's horses that grazed nearby, handing the reigns to his oldest brother. "Try not to lose this one," Dittmer joked, punching his brother in the shoulder. "Will I ever hear the end of this?" Abjörn sighed, shaking his head. His brothers all shared a glance before erupting into laughter. "Never," Sören answered.

The plan was set. Dittmer and Ryker would head east and start raiding the villages there, while Erik and Sören would head west. Once they had gathered everything they needed, they would regroup and prepare for the attack on Beecham's castle.

"Go get her brother," Sören laid a hand on Abjörn's shoulder. "I can see this is more than revenge for father," Sören said as the brothers shared a silent moment of reflection. Sima was to Abjörn as Firtha was to Sören. Once that thought had time to settle in Abjörn, he mounted his horse and headed after Sima.

The saddle felt strange. It was not because this horse was not as robust as his steed, it was because he could still feel Sima in his arms; the memory of her buttocks grinding on him, the taste of her lips, the smell on her neck. He smiled to himself as he thought back over her fearlessness and bravado. She was like no other woman he had met. An unknown force pulled him to her as surely as a siren's call.

Every time he closed his eyes, he saw her face, *I am a Viking. How has she done this to me?* he asked himself. Sima had invaded his mind, making it her home. He would not settle until he had her. All of her.

CHAPTER 9

DAYS HAD PASSED since Sima had arrived home. Her father wasn't pleased with her fleeing from the convent, and he was less pleased with the knowledge that she had escaped with a Viking. Sima was sure that Abjörn and his brothers had killed the soldiers sent to retrieve her. The fact was made ever so more apparent when they didn't return.

Every night since Sima arrived home, her dreams had been the same: a vivid re-enactment of her time with Abjörn. The memory of his lips on hers, the taste of his lips, and his beard caressing her skin. She could still feel it all. She longed for more.

She lay in bed tracing the path on her thigh where his fingers had trailed. Closing her eyes, she imagined her fingers were his. Her other hand stroked her nipples, which ached for his touch. She slid her fingers inside, letting her sweet nectar coat her hands. She moaned his name under her breath as she rubbed the throbbing bud between her legs. Even as she brought herself to climax and her body tingled and convulsed in response, it was not enough. No matter how many times she pleasured herself, the release was short-lived. Her body ached, wanting to feel his hands on her for real. To feel his long hot member between her legs. She had felt it on her back when they shared the saddle. She felt it against her knee when she kicked him, trying to escape. Curiosity drove her crazy. She wanted to see it, to handle it. To find out if it lived up to her imagination.

She thought about asking one of her father's guards to share her bed so that she could gain the release that was desperately needed. But she knew that too wouldn't be enough. She wanted to feel *his* weight on her.

She wanted her Viking back.

On the fourth night, her father came to her room to question Sima about her Viking. She gave what little information she had freely because she didn't believe the terrible things Abjörn had told her about her father. Her heart ached as the conversation continued, and while he didn't confirm Abjörn's accusations, Sima was smart enough to listen to the words her father chose not to say.

"Father, please tell me what he said isn't true? You're a man of honour. I can't believe you would do such things," she said, clinging to the loving memories of her father.

His expression didn't change. Instead, he looked at Sima with a stone face. "A lady shouldn't concern herself with such things," he said.

"Father?" she asked, but he waved her away, leaving her alone with her thoughts.

She sat down on her bed, thinking over everything that happened in the last week. She noticed a few changes in her father that she had chosen to ignore. He had become irritable, stressed, and easy to anger. But, on the other hand, he had always been open with Sima. Not once in all her years had he shied away from sharing information with her. Yet, she still had questions she needed answering from the night he sent her away.

And why had he sent away only me? Why did he not send my sisters too? Is he planning a marriage for me to another Lord's son? she asked herself. Eventually, her frustrations itched at her, she needed answers, and she wasn't going to stop until she got them.

She left her room and headed to her father's chamber. It was empty, so she wandered the halls, searching room after room. Finally, she came across the audience chamber. The door was open a crack, allowing light from the torches to dance through the gap.

She reached for the handle but stopped when she heard several voices inside. Her father was not alone.

"It's the best way to send your message, my Lord," one voice said.

"Have you managed to stop the raids?" her father asked.

"The villages to the east, yes. Last we heard, they have regrouped and are working the villages by the lake, west of the hills," another voice responded.

"You know what you must do. You have your orders," came a third voice. Sima stepped closer so she could hear more clearly.

"So, the settlement is empty?" her father asked.

"Apart from the women and children, yes. The last of the men left a day ago."

Sima searched her mind. She couldn't figure out to whom the other voices belonged. She thought they sounded familiar but could not recall the faces or names attached to them.

"Wait until nightfall. Use the shortcut through the valley as cover and burn the whole settlement to the ground. These savages need to know that this land is ours. If they want a war, we shall give it to them. Take anything of value and do what you want with anyone left behind," her father said.

Sima gasped, covering her mouth with her hand to not be discovered. *This is not honourable; this is cowardice. Innocent women and children will be slaughtered. I must warn Abjörn!* she thought, backing away from the door quickly.

She raced through the halls to her room to gather her cloak and a small bag she might need for supplies. Tears pricked her eyes. *This is not my father,* she thought, heartbroken by his betrayal. He had not just betrayed the truce with the Vikings, but he had betrayed her trust.

Tying her cloak tightly around her, she ran through the halls towards the kitchens. Sneaking out through the empty room, she slowly pushed the door to the courtyard open, trying not to let the hinges whine. Her father's guards had been patrolling the grounds continuously since she arrived home, and Sima didn't want to alert them. Instead, she needed to sneak past the guards in the courtyard and head to the stables.

Abjörn's horse was still there. Thankfully, he was a loyal steed who seemed to respond well to Sima. *If I give back his horse, perhaps he will listen to me, I need to make him hear,* she ducked behind a bush avoiding the two guards chatting away pacing the space between Sima and the stables.

Sliding past the stable doors, she grabbed a saddle that hung on the back wall to prepare the horse. As she turned in the dark, she bumped into something with such force that she stumbled, almost losing her footing before a hand grabbed her, keeping her steady. She squinted in the darkness, trying to see who was there with her. But, instead, the stranger pulled her closer, drawing her into the torchlight.

"Abjörn," she breathed.

"Lady Sima."

She grinned. Her Viking had come for her.

CHAPTER 10

"Do you have a problem with staying put? First the convent, then you take off with my horse," Abjörn asked with a grin. It felt good to be in her presence again, and his heart had beat harder when he felt her skin.

"Shush, there are guards outside; they will hear you," she whispered.

"Let them come," he said, once again not concerned by his volume.

"Abjörn, you don't understand you need to go home. My father is planning an attack. He has a small army. They will be leaving once the sun finally sets," Sima whispered in a panicked voice.

Abjörn shrugged, "my brothers and I can handle your father's men," he said, taking the saddle from her hands and placing it on the steed's back.

"No, Abjörn, you don't understand. They know all the women and children are unguarded. He plans on burning the settlement to the ground with everyone inside," she informed him.

He startled. He had not expected retaliation of this sort. Hastily, he readied the horse. While he would love nothing more than to spend more time with Sima, he needed to leave, if this was true. And fast. He considered the map in his mind trying to find the best route to collect his men and get them home as soon as possible.

Sima stood silently, waiting for Abjörn to respond. "Abjörn, please, you must do something," she insisted.

"I will. For starters, I'm taking back my horse," he said, taking the horse's reins and turning to leave. He pushed open the stable doors and mounted his steed. He took one last glance at her bosom as it heaved from her ragged breathing.

Sima grabbed his arm, sending fire through his veins at her touch. "They plan to cut through the valley. I know a quicker route through the woods. We can gather your brothers on the way and cut them off before they reach the settlement. Please take me with you. Please," she begged, tightening her grip.

Abjörn offered his hand, and when she took hold, he pulled her up in one quick movement and settled her in front of him in the saddle. It felt good to have her in his arms again. "Hold tight," he said, and she wrapped her arms as far around his thick frame as she could.

She buried her face in his chest, and he caught the scent of her hair. She smelled like roses and bluebells. Then, with one swift kick, the horse reared up, causing Sima to slide up into Abjörn and her grip to tighten. Abjörn grinned to himself. He had his woman back, and once they had stopped the attack on the settlement, he planned on taking her. His mind swam with all kinds of debauchery that he planned on indulging with her.

The horse charged out of the stables and ran through the courtyard, jumping over the stone wall circling the grounds as Abjörn directed him home. As the horse galloped along up and over the hills, Abjörn could feel Sima's breasts bouncing forth with the horse's rhythm. He kicked the steed's rib cage to make him run faster to enjoy the feel of her chest, imagining how it was nodding a little more vigorously with each movement.

Sima directed him over the hills towards the village. He knew his brothers and the rest of their forces were raiding. Once they arrived, Abjörn informed them of Lord Beecham's plan to burn down the settlement. Dittmer spat on the ground; his face flushed with anger. "What sort of coward attacks unarmed women and children? This man is more diabolical than we first thought. I can't wait to bury my axe in his skull."

Abjörn glanced over to Sima, who was obviously uncomfortable with the line of conversation. "Are you alright?" he asked her.

She nodded, but he knew she was lying. She lifted her gaze to meet his, "I don't like it, but you are right, he is a coward, and he needs to answer for his crimes. He must face the consequences of his actions," she said.

Sunset drew closer. If they didn't move fast, they wouldn't make it to the valley in time to stop the soldiers. "Erik, take Sima back home. The rest of you follow me and prepare for battle," Abjörn said, planting a kiss on Sima's forehead before he lifted her onto Erik's horse.

"Why do I have to miss out on all the fun?" Erik complained before doing as he was told.

Abjörn, his brothers, and the rest of their forces waited in the valley in ambush. Their archers hid in the trees while the rest of the troops lay in wait.

Lord Beecham's army had at least double the men that Abjörn had. But the brothers were not worried. When the soldiers were trapped, surrounded by Abjörn's men, he yelled "attack!" His voice, loud and booming, spooking birds out of the trees. Arrows flew through the air, singing on the wind before connecting with their targets. Abjörn and his men jumped out from hiding as swords clashed with swords, their blades slicing through skin and bone.

A chorus of pain and dying gasps echoed loudly. Such was the song of battle; how Abjörn loved it so. Abjörn searched the battlefield hoping to find Lord Beecham. But as he expected, the Lord was a coward who sent his men to battle alone, for he was nowhere in sight.

"Let us show Beecham what we Vikings can do," Sören roared over the crowd; with a swing of his axe, he took off a soldier's head, spinning around and hacking through another. Abjörn looked over to the trees to see Dittmer firing arrow after arrow, cutting down their enemies from above.

Ryker had stolen a horse and rode through the battlefield, slicing through anyone who stood in his way. Their armour was no match for the Viking's might.

Only a handful of Lord Beecham's men stood standing at the end of the battle. Abjörn was impressed with his men's fight. His men had stood firm with only a few minor injuries. Abjörn grabbed one of Lord Beecham's men by his collar, raising the man above his head. The soldier kicked, struggling to breathe in Abjörn's tight grasp.

"Take what is left of your men and go back to your master. Tell him what happens when he plans a cowardly attack on unarmed women and children," Abjörn stated, tossing the man to the ground. The soldier scrambled to his feet as what remained of the army jumped on horseback or ran away. "Tell your Lord if he wants a war with the Vikings, we will bring all the force of Asgärd with us," Abjörn yelled after them, his voice a roar of thunder to rival Thor.

His men cheered around him. "Abjörn, Abjörn, Abjörn," they chanted.

He smiled, pleased with their cheers, but wanting something else more than their accolades. "Come on, men, let's go home."

CHAPTER 11

Erik introduced Sima to Sören's wife, Firtha, whom Sima found that she got along with quite well. Firtha was so welcoming that it calmed Sima's nerves about the upcoming war.

Sima found the threat of impending danger mixed with adrenaline and the lust she carried, a titillating combination. She found she was more aroused than ever and wondered what would happen when Abjörn arrived home.

The word surprised her. She thought it again. *Home.* It felt right calling this place *home.* She had always felt out of place in the King's court. And her father's betrayal cut like a knife.

Firtha burst through the hut and a smile of delight spread over her face. "Sima, they are back, come quickly," she said, grabbing Sima's hand and pulling her outside. Sima ran behind Firtha as the Viking men rode into the settlement to the sound of their cheering women.

Their arrival was met with a feast, followed by drinking and dancing around campfires. For the first time in her life, Sima felt she had found where she belonged. She had more in common with the women here than she ever did back in the King's court.

Later that night, Abjörn and Sima sat together in his hut. *Their* hut. "My father will come looking for me," Sima said, sipping on the last of her mead.

"Let him," Abjörn said, removing his tunic and furs, allowing Sima the first look at the wall of muscle she had spent many an hour fantasising about. It was just as Sima had dreamed. Chiselled muscle decorated with a scar or two that just added to its beauty.

"If he came looking, would you want me to leave with him?" she asked, testing the waters.

Abjörn didn't disappoint. "Let him try and take you from me," Abjörn replied, stepping closer to her, and stroking the exposed part of her shoulder.

"So, you don't want me to leave?" she asked, allowing her shaking hand to stroke just above his hip.

"Do you want to leave?" Abjörn asked. Sima locked eyes with his and shook her head gently.

"What do you want?" he asked, wrapping his hand around her waist, and pulling her close.

Sima bit her lip as she gazed up at him. "I want to stay here...with you," she breathed.

A slight smirk creased the corners of Abjörn's lips. "What else do you want, Sima?" he asked, running his free hand through her hair.

She closed her eyes, remembering the feeling from the last time his fingers were entangled in her hair. She hooked her fingers into the waistline of his trousers, pushing them down, exposing the part of him she wanted most. She marvelled at the beauty between his legs. It was long and thick, with a slight curve to the left.

"Is this how ladies of the court always act?" Abjörn asked, stepping out of his trousers.

"Is this how Viking ladies act?" she asked, slowly unlacing her bodice, freeing her breasts one inch at a time.

Abjörn chuckled and nodded in response. "Viking women are strong-willed and unafraid to ask for what they want," Abjörn replied, his eyes following the line of her fingers.

"Then I guess I was never meant to be a Lady of the court... I'm meant to be a Viking woman," she breathed, allowing her dress to fall at her feet.

Abjörn gripped her hair once more in the forceful yet gentle way she had longed for and brought his lips down to hers. His tongue plundered her lips as she opened her mouth to welcome him.

His hands cupped her round buttocks as he picked her up, allowing her to wrap herself around him as he carried her over to the table.

He sat her on edge and dropped to his knees, spreading her legs open wide. Sima rested her hands behind her on the table to support herself and draped her legs over Abjörn's shoulders. She felt his breath warm her inner thigh as he trailed kisses upwards until he came to explore the part of her that ached for his touch.

She let out a moan of pleasure as his tongue lapped over the aching bud. This was better than she had ever imagined. As his tongue worked its magic, his fingers spread her lips apart and stretched her wide. Sima allowed herself to lay back on the table as her hands explored her breasts, stroking and pinching her aching nipples. Her breathing quickened as he brought her closer and closer to the ecstasy she craved. "Abjörn, yes!" she moaned, panting as the pressure grew.

Finally, he sent her over the edge, and she screamed his name. Sima jumped off the table, taking his hands in hers, and guided him over to the bed. He lay down, and Sima straddled herself over his hips. She wanted to ride him, to feel him deep inside her.

She took his hard cock in her hand and guided it into her, sucking in a breath as he filled her completely. She let out a moan. He felt so good inside her.

Abjörn rested his hands on her hips as she slowly slid up and down him, adjusting to his length. Sima hadn't been with many men, but Abjörn was more significant than all of them. As she picked up speed, grinding her hips, their moans of ecstasy grew until both were gasping for breath. She could feel her climax brewing deep inside of her, but she didn't want to feel her release until he reached his. Instead, she wanted to feel his release inside her. His hands reached up and massaged her breasts as they moaned louder. "Oh, Abjörn," she cried.

"Sima," he growled as his release took over, and Sima finally allowed herself to feel her own release with him, squeezing herself around him feeling every inch. Eventually, she fell to his chest, panting, the sound of his heartbeat like a lullaby as his arms wrapped lovingly around her.

That was better than any fantasy, she thought before drifting off to sleep in his arms.

EPILOGUE

ABJÖRN GATHERED his family to him.

"Lord Beecham may not be our only problem," Abjörn said as he sat at the table with his brothers, shortly joined by Sima.

Abjörn nodded to Sima. She took a deep breath and said, "My father does not act alone. I believe he is acting on the orders of someone higher, maybe someone closer to the King."

"So was his attack on the settlement his idea or someone else's?" Dittmer asked, a look of confusion on his face.

"I do not know. My father lost the land the settlement sits on before I was born. So, I am unsure who owned them before the King gave you the land," Sima said.

"So, we now have another enemy," Ryker said, his expression sombre.

"No matter how many enemies we have in this strange land, we have Odin on our side and will not be defeated," Abjörn said.

THE END

ERIK

HUMBLED BY THE RUNEMASTER

PROLOGUE

THE JÜRGENSEN BROTHERS sat in the council hut. They had sat talking for so long, their stomachs had now begun to rumble. Abjörn, being the oldest son, was considered the wisest, but even with his counsel and wisdom, they were all no closer to figuring out who Lord Beecham was in leagues with.

Tempers began to flare as the conversation went round in circles. Frustration lay thick in the air.

"You are making no sense, brother. We discussed this already!" groaned Abjörn, rubbing his bearded face in frustration.

Erik struggled to control his temper. Being the second son, he was not in line to inherit anything, and he had had to fight harder and learn faster than all the rest to prove his worth. Every idea Erik had was quickly shot down by his older brother, making Erik look foolish and feeling resentful towards Abjörn.

The hut rumbled as everyone fought to lead the conversation and hear their ideas. Sören rubbed his temples as a new headache started to take hold.

A thought occurred to Ryker as he finally asked a question that no one had considered before. "What was father doing over here in England in the first place?"

The question silenced the room. The question was so obvious that the brothers looked around at each other, silently questioning why no one had thought of it sooner.

In truth, their father's journey here didn't make much sense. As someone in direct line to the Danish throne, it was strange that he would put himself in danger by attempting a raiding expedition himself.

Erik gave the question some serious thought; there was a lot to consider that none of them had realised before. "Ryker is right; Father had not attempted any expedition in years. He'd had far too many other important duties to attend to." Erik stood up to give his argument more merit. "Why attempt this one? On such strange shores and without his guard, and also without us?"

Abjörn chewed on his brother's words, rubbing his beard as his brow furrowed, trying to come up with an answer. He could not.

The room fell into a more resounding silence as no one else could answer the question. Their father trusted them all implicitly, often sending them on expeditions he deemed too dangerous to attempt himself. His sons were strong, intelligent men with many successful battles under their belts. While past royals kept a tight war council, their father had entrusted them against his royal advisor's wishes.

The question lay thick in the air, weighing down heavily on all the brothers. Finally, as night drew close, with no answers or new avenues of enquiry to follow, Abjörn excused the council for the evening.

As the men left the hut, those who had found wives were met with open arms—greetings of embraces and passionate kisses before each couple headed to their humble abodes.

Erik watched, perplexed, as the questions of that evening still swam in his mind, plaguing him. If Abjörn could not find an answer, he must. If he could figure out the reason for his father's journey, then maybe his brothers would see how wise he indeed was.

He watched the love-drunk couples head off to their huts, and he shook his head. No wonder none of them could develop any viable answers or plans; they were all drunk on their women. Women made you soft. Thank Odin, he still had his wits about him, he thought.

Erik trudged through the settlement, the weight of his mind

pressing him down and making his blood boil as he struggled to find the answers he sought.

His hut was furthest away from his brothers; he preferred it that way. Erik liked to avoid the sounds of his brothers' nightly antics. As he drew closer to his hut, one of the women who had recently come of age and made it known how much she hoped to find a husband, called to him softly.

Erik was not short of female admirers, but as with all previous women's attempts to gain his attention, he ignored her. Instead, he looked over and snarled, disgust filling him. He had far more important things to do than being tied up in a female entanglement.

The young woman fluttered her skirts and exposed one of her nipples in an attempt to entice him. Beautiful as she was, he continued to ignore her.

He had come here to prove himself, grow his fortune, and build a future for himself. He had come to show his worth. His mission would never change. He would not stop until his mission was complete. The answers must lie with his father.

There was a place to go when a man needed answers, and the answers were closer than he thought. He must go to Bryn.

CHAPTER 1

BRYN HAD BEEN A WARRIOR ONCE, a warrior just as strong and fierce as any man. She had never wanted to rely on a man to get her anything she needed. Even as a girl, Bryn had been ferociously independent and often beat the boys her age when playing raid.

Bryn often looked back at her time in battle with a fondness, closely followed by sorrow. Her last battle had been one for the ages. And while she did herself and her father proud, she had been severely injured. Her leg had never completely healed. The injured appendage now sat in an odd position from the knee down, making her walk with a prominent limp.

Pain had always been her friend; she never shied away from it, and she dealt with it as well as any man. Yet even in her new life, she often thought her friend, pain, had rather overstayed its welcome.

She would never ride into battle again, so Bryn had been forced to dedicate her life to her other talents. Thankfully, Bryn had received a magical gift sent from Frigg, the Queen of Asgärd, and highest of the goddesses. Bryn used this gift as the settlement's Runemaster.

Bryn's leg was giving her a lot of trouble that eve; she was about to drink some milk of the poppy and retire for the evening when the second Jürgensen brother barged into her tent.

"You are the Runemaster, yes?" Erik asked, his face stern. For a second, his question sounded more like an accusation.

"Aye, I am; what do you need?" Bryn asked, hobbling across the tent to the table containing everything she needed for rune casting.

Erik looked around her tent as if he had fallen behind enemy lines. Bryn knew that look. Often, when people asked her to cast, it was because they believed or at least wanted to believe; however, a handful thought her gifts to be an act of fraud.

"What answers do you seek?" Bryn asked, walking slower, trying to ignore the stabbing pain in her hip. She clenched her jaw, reaching out to grab at her chair, allowing herself to take the weight off her injury finally. "I need answers about my father and his journey here as things do not add up. I must figure out the answer to our problem," Erik said, moving across the room to sit with Bryn.

Erik leaned back in the chair and stared intently at Bryn. "I need the runes to tell me what was so special about this expedition to make father travel without giving us any word. I need to know who our enemy is working with."

Bryn was momentarily stunned. She looked back at him blankly, scanning his face for any hint of knowing. Then, after a few moments, she realised. He didn't know.

With everything that Bryn knew, not just from secrets told to her when people come to seek her guidance in casting runes, but from her history in battle, she knew enemies were everywhere. She also knew sometimes foes were disguised as friends.

Erik looked back at her, oblivious to the thoughts running around in her mind. If Bryn did say so herself, he was a beautiful specimen of a man. Thick blonde hair, muscles upon muscles, and high chiselled cheekbones. He had a strong jaw framed with a long blonde beard, which had two small braids dangling down past his chin. There was a slight scar across his left cheek and blue eyes so light they were almost grey.

He looked like the embodiment of Thor himself, Bryn thought, as his brow furrowed, impatient.

Erik was growing concerned at Bryn's silence. As his brow deepened, she noticed another scar through his right eyebrow. His reputation as a fearsome warrior preceded him.

Shaking her head, trying to shake off the sudden unfamiliar feelings of attraction, the longer he looked at her with the brooding look, the stronger her pulse raced. She mustn't allow attraction to cloud her sight, she told herself, before abruptly standing up and pushing herself away from the table.

"I'm sorry, I cannot help you; the answers you seek are not mine to give. Please leave," she answered, turning away from him.

She stood fiddling with trinkets on the wooden shelves she had erected at the back of her tent and waited for the sound of him leaving.

CHAPTER 2

Erik left the tent, an uneasy feeling settling over him. The answers were not hers to give; what could she mean by that? The Jürgensen brothers were Danish royalty, and whatever she meant, Erik was not used to anyone saying no to him. People often said yes purely because of his royal blood, fear while he was raiding, or just admiration for his wins in battle. 'No' was not usually a word Erik heard. The more he tossed the thought around in his mind, the more frustrated he felt.

How dare she refuse him, he thought, as he quickly turned on his heels and headed back to her tent.

Erik entered the Runemaster's tent with as much force as was possible in the fabric structure. He whipped his head around to find Bryn working on a runic carving. The large stone tablet was the most prominent thing in the tent aside from him. He didn't realise how he hadn't noticed it before.

She continued to tap away at the stone, and he took a few more steps inside.

"Why do you refuse to cast for me? What are you hiding? I demand answers; I am a Jürgensen brother. Do you know whom you refuse?" he bellowed, pacing the small space as his blood raged.

The Runemaster ignored him, continuing to tap away as if he wasn't there.

Erik's anger grew the more she ignored his demands. He stamped his foot like a petulant child in an attempt to gain her attention. But once again, she didn't flinch at his presence.

"I asked you a question!" he snarled.

"You asked me several, in fact," she started, blowing dust from her carving. "And yes, Erik Jürgensen, I know exactly who you are... Do you know who I am?"

She tapped away at the lowest part of the stone. Erik fell quiet for a moment, annoyed that she dared question him, but not wanting to look foolish, he stubbornly answered.

"You are the Runemaster," he said, his remark sounding more like a question to his ears.

"We already know that now, don't we?" she said, and Erik could hear the amusement in her voice. She was taunting him. He had never been teased by a woman before; the only ones to taunt him were his brothers. It was a feeling he didn't like.

"Of course, you would not know who I am. A warrior like yourself would never pay someone with an imperfection like mine a second glance. You have never paid me a moment's thought before this eve," she tutted, slowly rising to stand. "Wanting answers but not even bothering to ask my name."

Erik noticed how she struggled with her leg and admired how she still seemed strong. He watched her as she examined her work, stroking each rune, checking it was perfect.

He thought over her accusation for a moment before gently offering his response. "Your name is Bryn, and your limp is not the reason I have not noticed you. I do not notice women; it is only when they throw themselves at my feet when I am left with no choice but to notice them."

"Ah, then you do not rise at the sight of women; perhaps it is your fellow warriors who get you to rise?" She smirked, finally glancing over her shoulder, catching his gaze. Her remark did not faze Erik. He had more important things to think about than women and the dramas that came with them.

"Ha! You taunt me with words that have no effect. Trust when I say, I have no issue with rising when the mood allows!" he laughed, folding his arms across his broad chest, and cocking an eyebrow at her.

Erik let his eyes cast Bryn over. She spoke some truth, he had never noticed her before, and looking at her now, he realised how much of a mistake that was. She was different from the other woman in the settlement. She had the essence of a warrior. She was strong with muscular arms and shoulders while still slender and feminine. Her curves were very pleasing to the eye.

Her eyes were harsh, almost angry at the world, but Erik could see past what her eyes hid. Her eyes were nearly the same shade as his. Her hair also almost matched the shade of blonde that was his own. She had it braided in several places on top of her head, Erik assumed to keep it from falling into her eyes, and the rest fell in waves down her back. Erik wondered how those locks would feel wrapped around his fingers during the throws of passion. The thought alone gave him cause to rise, making him shift uneasily from foot to foot.

"Ah, then you fear my magic," she taunted, smirking as she slowly turned to face him, a mischievous glint in her eyes.

Erik reared up at her words, instantly forgetting the images of passion that rolled around in his mind only moments before. Being accused of only rising at the sight of his fellow warriors didn't bother him, but an accusation of fear? That he would not let stand!

Erik prided himself on being a fearless warrior. He had far too much to prove to let fear ever stand in his way. His brow creased, and he took a step closer to her with every word he spoke until he towered over her.

"I am afraid of nothing; you will never meet a warrior as free from fear as I. Your sex does not scare me, your imperfection, as you so call it, does not scare me, and your runes do not scare me. Would you care for a demonstration?" he asked as she stood with her back against her stone carving.

He expected her to bow down against his size as he towered over her not just in height but in muscle. But, instead, she stood firm, unmoving, as she glared back deep into his eyes. While her face and mouth refused to answer, Erik was sure that her eyes spoke to him.

Erik pushed forward, pinning Bryn between him and her carving.

She pressed her hands into his chest, trying to put distance between them, but Erik grabbed both her wrists in one of his massive hands and pinned them above her head, leaving Bryn at her mercy.

He brought down his lips on hers, pushing his tongue into her mouth and exploring it. He wasn't surprised to feel her body respond as her tongue massaged his in response.

He allowed his free hand to explore her curves, and he distinctly heard her moan with pleasure at his touch. He reached down to explore beneath her skirts, stroking the thigh of her injured leg when Bryn suddenly had a change of heart.

With a force Erik was not expecting – and was quite impressed by – Bryn pulled her hands free and pushed him hard in the chest, forcing him to take a step back. She grabbed the long staff she used to assist her in walking and used it to balance herself as she brought up her good leg and kicked Erik hard in the stomach, making him stumble back and gasp as the hit forced the air from his lungs.

As Erik rubbed his stomach, he let out a chuckle, amused by the Runemaster's change of heart. He glanced up at her and her face twisted in anger. Grabbing her staff, she spun fast, swinging her staff at Erik. It connected hard with his cheek, and he dropped to his knees, and before he could retaliate or assess what had just occurred, she swung her staff again, knocking him flat on his stomach.

"Give me one good reason why I shouldn't castrate you here and now!" she barked, glaring down at Erik as he sat up, rubbing his jaw.

"You didn't seem to be complaining; in fact, I can still taste your tongue on my lips," Erik chuckled. His response met with another swing of her staff and a swift unsheathing of a small blade from her boot.

Erik knelt still as Bryn held the blade to his throat. The pair stared deeply into each other's eyes, each sizing the other up. Erik watched her eyes twitch and smirked a little more. Bryn had been aroused; she had been enjoying herself, even if she denied it now.

Both Erik and Bryn still gently panted for breath after their shared kiss, but both were stubborn, and neither wanted to be the first to break eye contact.

"Now I have proved I am not afraid or repulsed by you, will you cast your runes and answer my questions?" he asked.

Bryn trembled lightly as her grip on the blade tightened; she glared at Erik a second longer before stuffing the knife back in her boot and standing back to her full height.

The anger on her face was unmoving. Silently, she moved over to her table and, with furrowed brows, indicated Erik should sit with her. Erik stood and slowly joined her at the table, keeping a close and amused eye on her.

"I will cast for you, but only because my duty compels me to. Once the reading is complete, you will leave and never bother me again," she said firmly, picking up her runes and casting them wide across the table in between them both.

CHAPTER 3

BRYN LOOKED over the small runestones that lay across the wood, trying to concentrate as her heart still raced. There was a mix of arousal and hatred for the man sitting in front of her.

She kept a steady eye on the runes, being careful not to let her gaze drift up to meet his. She couldn't stand to look at him, conflicted by the feelings stirring in her and her anger and pride.

"The runes point to Denmark," she uttered, scanning over the tiles carefully.

She had not expected her casting to reveal anything like what sat before her. They all but named the man behind the betrayal of the late future King of Denmark.

Bryn knew that she needed to tread carefully. Erik was clearly a passionate man, be it with a woman or when it came to his mission. Bryn knew if she gave too much information too soon, it might lead Erik down the wrong path. She didn't want his anger to get him hurt.

"What do you see?" he asked, leaning forward closer to the runes as if he would suddenly be able to read them too.

"The runes speak of a threat from familiar shores," she began. "The alliance between these lands and home is an alliance of enemies, not friends." The concern in her voice was hard to mask.

Everything makes sense now, she thought as she looked over the stone tiles once more. She knew more than she expected, and now her heart began to race for entirely different reasons than before. If her conclusions were correct, things were a lot worse than they seemed. Should she tell him? He needed to know, they all did. But if she spoke, would she be putting them in danger?

She argued with herself, too scared to say the words out loud. The enemy the runes warned of was her enemy too, and the fight was getting closer to home.

"What do you mean? Our enemies fight together?" Erik asked.

Bryn looked over the casting on the table once more, reading what lay before her over and over to make sure she had got it right.

She couldn't hold this back any longer. She took a deep breath and sat up straight, finally looking Erik in the eye. He looked back, waiting anxiously for her answer. She opened her mouth to speak when the casting was interrupted by shouting from outside.

"A ship with friendly sails. It is the Jarl!" bellowed the voice outside.

Bryn's heart began to race. It still scared her once in a while how accurately she could interpret the tiles, and now she would have to reveal what she knew before it was too late.

Erik stood to leave, and Bryn grabbed his sleeve tightly in her fist. He looked at his sleeve, then back at her face, confused as to why she felt the need to stop him. She could still feel his kiss on her lips, and her fingers tingled as she touched him. Conflicting emotions flooded her as his eyes met hers once again.

"Do not leave; I still have much to tell you. I fear it is of great importance," she said, but Erik refused to listen.

"The Jarl is here; he will have come with much-needed supplies and more men. I must go help my brothers," he said before he ran from her tent.

Bryn looked over the tiles once more, taking stock of their message before clearing them away. As she cleared the last tile away, she slammed her fist into the table, anger and frustration washing over her like the waves the Jarl sailed in on.

"He demands a casting and then flees before I finish. Why seek my guidance and then reject the results?" she breathed.

She was unsure what frustrated her more, his rejection of her reading, his manhandling of her, or that fact that she wanted more. He had been right, she did enjoy his touch, but she knew it could be dangerous to allow him the power of knowing he was right.

CHAPTER 4

THE SETTLEMENT ERUPTED into celebration at the ship's arrival. The thought of the Jarl arriving gave great cause for excitement.

Bryn hobbled through the settlement, dodging excitement as others rushed by. Fires were started, and a huge celebration feast was prepared. Bryn watched as the Jarl and his men travelled ashore and were greeted by the Jürgensen brothers.

That night, once their guests had settled in after their long journey, the feast began. Women and children danced around the fires, barrels of mead and ale and wine were cracked open, and warriors battled to show off their strength to the Jarl. Practise fights ensued with wooden children's swords and arm wrestling.

Bryn scoffed; it sickened her how people would fall at the man's feet as if he were better than the rest.

He is nothing special; even with my leg, I could beat him in battle, she thought, watching Erik intently, listening to the excitement within the camp.

"Now the Jarl has arrived, we have enough forces to take Lord Beecham and anyone else who stands in our way," slurred a drunken voice in the crowds.

Bryn was used to no one paying her much attention, and right now, she was thankful for the fact. She pulled the hood of her cloak over her head and tried to blend into the shadows.

She must speak with Erik but trying to distract him from the guest of honour, the Jarl Halfden, was going to be a task. Everyone clung to his every word.

Bryn paced – as best she could – every cell in her body stinging with frustration as she listened to the conversation between Halfden and the Jürgensen brothers. Halfden urged the brothers to continue the attack on Lord Beecham and suggested raiding further north, expanding on the treaty's limits.

"The betrayal of the Scots makes any boundaries set forth by the treaty moot. We can now take what is rightfully ours," Halfden slurred as he emptied yet another glass of ale.

"The Jarl is right; Lord Beecham is not the only one to betray us. We must repay that betrayal in blood," boomed Sören.

Erik, Abjörn, Sören, Ryker and Dittmer, all agreed with the Jarl.

Bryn stopped dead in her tracks as her blood ran cold. This was madness; she must speak with Erik. He needed to hear the rest of the casting. She could not lie to him anymore. He needed to know what she did. *But how*? How could she pull him away from the Jarl? She battled with herself.

Laughter nearby gave Bryn a possible answer to her problem. She looked up and found Firtha, the wife of Sören, playing with some children.

Firtha was known for being a strong woman, and as someone else gifted with magic, Bryn could think of no one else she would trust to help her. She staggered over and bowed her head in greeting.

"Firtha, may I speak with you?" she asked.

Firtha turned to Bryn and gently dismissed the children. She eyed Bryn at first with suspicion, and then a smile spread across her face.

"Bryn, isn't it?" Firtha asked, "The Runemaster?"

Bryn nodded and stepped a little closer. She knew she could trust Firtha, but that didn't mean she would. She told Firtha only what she thought she needed to know and only enough that the information would not reach the wrong hands if anyone else were listening.

"I must speak with Erik; it is of great importance. We have unfinished business," Bryn whispered, leaning heavily on her walking staff.

Firtha eyed Bryn a knowing smirk played across her lips. "What sort of unfinished business?" Firtha smiled, nudging Bryn in the arm.

"This is not the time or place," Bryn replied.

Firtha laughed and nodded happily. "I will help you, Runemaster Bryn."

Firtha took hold of Bryn's hand and slowly led her to camp's other side.

CHAPTER 5

"THE NIGHT GROWS OLD, and I have drunk enough. Jarl Halfden, it is an honour to have you here with us, but I must depart," Erik slurred as his brothers laughed and clapped him around the shoulder.

They all shared a loving brotherly embrace before Erik staggered with blurry eyes back to his hut.

Erik hummed a tune of war from home in Denmark as he took shaky steps towards his hut in their new land. One day, they would sing tales of his victories, he thought to himself.

The evening had Erik's blood swimming with adrenaline. The upcoming battles would give him plenty of opportunities to prove himself, to become the man his father would have been proud of. He wondered which of his forthcoming battles would become a ballad that the bards would sing with pride and honour as he dined in the halls of Vallhalla.

Erik entered his hut, still humming and singing under his breath. He began to disrobe, removing his tunic and tossing it to the floor when the sounds of his bed creaking caught his attention. He snapped his head upright, not expecting the sight he saw.

Bryn was perched on the end of his cot, leaning on her walking staff. He wondered how long she had been there and noticed how she hadn't attempted to announce her presence while he disrobed. He looked her over and saw how she eyed him fondly, her eyes wandering over his broad chest of solid muscle.

"Runemaster, to what do I owe the pleasure?" Erik asked. She stood, and he noticed how she had already removed her cloak. So, she either wanted what he wanted or had been waiting for a while.

"I need to speak with you. I need to finish the task we started," she answered.

Erik watched as she took a step towards him; he admired her form even more.

"What we started? I like the sound of that," he breathed, sliding his hand around her waist and pulling her to him. Her scent was intoxicating as he ran his nose along her collar bone.

"Erik, I need to complete your reading," she said, sinking into his touch as his lips grazed her skin.

"The reading can wait. You stir something in me, Runemaster, and right now, all I can think about is the memory of your lips on mine, the taste of you. I wonder how the rest of you tastes."

His hands reached up into her hair, and their mouths clashed in a kiss of passion.

"Erik…" Bryn breathed as his hands slid down her waist and around her back, cupping her backside as he lifted her and wrapped her legs around his waist.

He carried her over to a chair by the fireplace. He sat himself down and sat Bryn astride his lap. He lay kisses down her neck and collar bone. His hands reached up her back to untie her clothes as he pulled them down past her shoulders, exposing her breasts. She breathed his name once more as his mouth explored her.

"Yes, Bryn, do you feel me rise for you now?" he groaned, gently taking a fist full of her hair and pulling her head back, giving him free access to the parts of her that drove him mad with desire.

Passion filled the room, a desire the pair had never experienced before nor thought they ever wanted. But they both sat exploring each other, tasting one another, soaking up every second of pleasure.

"Come, Runemaster, let us finish what we started," he groaned in her ear, nibbling on her lobe. He wrapped his arms around her and lifted her, preparing to carry her to his bed.

She had been groaning and moaning her pleasure; she had been speaking his name in the throes of passion. He liked how it sounded on her tongue, and he wanted to hear more of it. To listen to her scream his name as he thrust himself inside her.

His mind flashed with all the ways he planned on pleasuring her and all the ways he intended for her to please him. His cock pulsed at the thought, but before he could enjoy the pleasures his mind had created, Bryn yelled.

"The Jarl is in alliance with the Scottish Lord who killed your father!"

CHAPTER 6

ERIK SUMMONED HIS BROTHERS, and they met in secret with their wives. They all waited patiently; Erik had been vague with his request. Bryn stood firm beside Erik, the pair refusing to look at each other, not speaking a word about the encounter that still had their nerve-endings firing like lightning.

"Why must we huddle in shadows, brother?" asked Sören.

His wife eyed Bryn with a mischievous glint. Bryn fought back a smirk; Firtha had been right. Despite Bryn's better judgment, she did have an attraction to Erik.

"The Runemaster...Bryn, she has information she needed to share, information about father," Erik said, nodding to Bryn for her to speak.

She stood forward and began her story. "My father travelled with yours, they fought together many a time, and when your father insisted on making this trip, mine insisted on travelling with him."

She paused. "I, too, was left in the dark about the expedition until it was too late." There was a catch in her throat as her chest heaved. "Unfortunately, my father died on this trip too."

Bryn looked around the room. "My father was never one to hide things from me, so he left me a message. A message in the runes tells me what had really happened that day... The King himself had sent the runes."

She watched as everyone listened to her every word and waited for her to continue. "The King suspected that the Jarl was taking money from the Danegeld, but when the ships first landed here, they met with a man who would later become the Jarl, and they also met the local lord, Beecham."

She watched as, piece by piece, everyone put her story together. She glanced over to Erik, who nodded, encouraging her to continue.

"The runes did not tell the whole story. The runes never do; we cannot be given all the answers. If that were the case, we would never learn." She glanced again at Erik, she knew he still wanted more precise answers, but even with her knowledge, she didn't have the answers he needed.

"The Jarl's sudden arrival here is shadowed in darkness. Since becoming the Jarl, he has not once visited the settlement. He has not helped us grow; he knows not of what troubles we have encountered or friends we have gained and lost. Yet he comes here encouraging further war?"

Bryn's gut twisted, and her warrior senses told her that she needed to be on guard. There was a foul plot afoot, and she had somehow got mixed up in it. She wondered if this could be a chance for her to be a warrior once more.

"You speak in riddles, Runemaster, and riddles that make no sense. The Jarl is here to help us. He brings supplies; he brings much-needed numbers to help us," Dittmer stated, only to be silenced by Abjörn raising his hand.

"Dittmer is right. The Jarl is our friend, our ally; perhaps you read the tiles wrong, from what I believe, you were not always a runemaster," Abjörn said.

Bryn glanced at Erik; his brother's words appeared to anger him.

"Don't be dense, brother. Help us with what? Before his arrival here, he did not know our troubles, had any one of you sent a message to him asking for aid?" Erik glanced around. "Where did he get the information from?"

Bryn stood a little taller, glancing up at Erik with a feeling close to pride. He was fighting with her. It surprised her that he chose to side with her, but it also surprised her how much she liked the thought of him at her side.

"Bryn is right; it is suspect that he arrives now, and on his first night here, he encourages war. Tell me, brother, if it was anyone else, would you not treat them with the same suspicion?" Erik asked, stepping closer to Bryn.

He now stood so close she could feel his warmth; she found it oddly arousing and comforting.

"While you have a point, I do not see why the King would choose to say nothing when father died," Ryker interrupted.

"None of us thought it was odd that father travelled out on this voyage alone after all those years. Why would the King? Likely he just believed that father's death was a result of ill luck while on a raid," Erik spoke.

Sima, the wife of Erik's older brother and the daughter of their enemy, Lord Beecham, had sat silently listening. She stood and took a step forward towards Bryn, a look of confusion and conflict across her face.

"The Jarl is what the English would call an Earl, am I right?" she asked.

Bryn nodded her response.

"What is his name?" Sima asked,

"Halfden," Abjörn answered.

Sima's eyes widened, and she spun around to face her husband. She, too, had information that would be deemed significant. "I know that name; I have heard it before in my father's court. I can't remember why, but I remember the name. Bryn speaks the truth; what if this Jarl Halfden is the one from whom my father takes his orders? What if this is all part of their plan? I think there is a bigger plot we do not see yet," Sima said.

The group passed ideas around, and potential theories while piecing together the information they had gathered until the sun was due to rise.

They decided that they needed more information before they could make a move. Action too soon could result in catastrophe. It was better to tread with caution and make a move when the time was right. The final decision was to watch and wait. A decision that no one was particularly fond of.

CHAPTER 7

"BRYN, your counsel tonight has proven to be most valuable. I was mistaken to discount you. Would you like to join me for a drink before the sunrise?" Erik asked, hoping Bryn would accept his invitation.

He had never looked twice at any woman, but he was beginning to see Bryn in a new light, and he wanted to spend time getting to know her more.

"The sun will greet us soon, but I will happily share the rest of the evening with you," she replied with a smile as she followed him back to his hut.

Erik would have customarily covered the distance in a couple of strides, but he slowed down to keep pace with Bryn. He watched her closely and noticed how she barely let her limp affect her, but also how her eyes indicated a twinge of pain every couple of steps. Still, she never once complained, and Erik admired her strength.

They arrived at his hut, and Erik realised he didn't know how to act around her. He had never been interested in women, and the ones he knew were nothing like Bryn.

He pulled out a chair for her to sit on, and she eyed him with a twinge of annoyance, refusing the chair and insisting on sitting in the chair closest to the fireplace.

He went to his secret stash of mead and poured them both a drink.

He handed the beverage to Bryn, who accepted it happily. They sat in silence for a few moments. Bryn could feel Erik's eyes on her.

"Why do you insist on watching me?" she asked with a slight grin.

"In truth? I find you fascinating; it's rare anyone can best me, and you put me flat on my belly in three strikes," he spoke honestly.

His words stunned Bryn. She had no idea how to react and was even more surprised when Erik continued.

"I find when I am with you, I am not myself; it's an odd feeling, and I don't know what to do with it," he said, simply taking another sip of his drink.

Bryn was uncomfortable with the line of conversation. No man had ever spoken to her as softly and honestly as Erik. Leaving her staff by the fire, she limped around the room, admiring all of Erik's possessions and giving her attention to everything in the room except Erik.

"May I ask you a question?" Erik asked.

"What answers do you seek?" she answered, assuming he wanted her for her skills.

Erik stood and joined her across the room. She felt him behind her and turned slowly, craning her neck to look up at him.

He shook his head. "No, I do not ask for help from the Runes. Instead, I want to ask *you* a question."

Bryn swallowed, afraid of where this was headed, and hobbled back to her seat. Erik watched her closely, and she nodded her consent to ask.

"How did you injure your leg?" Erik asked.

Bryn was not expecting that to be the question he asked. Although it was usually a topic that she had no problem retelling, at that moment, in front of Erik Jürgensen, she felt more vulnerable and exposed than she ever had in battle. She opened her mouth to speak but found her throat had become dry, and she could not say.

Erik saw her discomfort and knelt at her feet; he rested a hand on her knee and looked up at her softly. "I am sorry. I did not mean to offend."

Bryn pushed his hand away and stood abruptly to her feet, trying to hide the fact that the sudden change in position had her wobbling.

"I do not want or need your pity," she spat, her pulse racing.

Erik stayed on his knees, looking up at her in complete confusion.

"I was a fearsome shieldmaiden. I was hurt in battle; that is all you need to know," she answered, looking straight ahead as if looking out over the horizon.

"I was not offering you my pity," Erik smirked as he stood once again to his full height.

Once he stood tall, Bryn had no choice but to meet his gaze, for he towered over her like a giant oak tree.

"Bryn, the Runemaster, I do not doubt that you are a fearsome warrior. I have experienced your strength first hand. Pity is one thing you will never get from me. I will, however, offer my admiration and respect; if you would accept that," he breathed.

They stared deep into each other's ice-blue eyes, their breath increasing, in sync with each other.

The tension between them grew with every second. Then, all at once, the two came together in a kiss of aggressive passion. They explored each other with their hands, grabbing and pulling, trying to bring the other closer. They were lost in the throes of passion as they tore at each other's clothes.

Bryn let her hands stroke the muscle of Erik's chest; it was firmer than she thought. Erik's brought his mouth down, taking Bryn's breast in his mouth, nibbling and sucking at her nipples. She let out a moan of pleasure and pushed him back. Then, keeping her eyes locked with his, she sank to her knees as she brought down his trousers, freeing him.

She was amazed at the sight; he was long and thick, and he pulsed in her hand as she took hold of him. Then, keeping her eyes locked on his, she took him in her mouth.

Erik sucked in a breath through his teeth as Bryn rolled her tongue around his length. She sucked his length, and Erik felt his knees grow weak. "Bryn," he moaned as he watched her worship him, in a way no woman had pleased him before.

She was truly something magnificent, he thought. He felt himself growing harder. He didn't want to finish, not yet.

Erik pulled back and scooped Bryn up, carrying her over to the table. He spun her around and lifted her skirt. He reached around to cup her breasts and thrust himself inside in one swift movement. She was already wet, ready to receive him.

"Erik," she moaned; he filled her so completely, that she had never felt anything like him before. She sighed and cried in ecstasy as he stretched her. She felt herself building with each of his powerful thrusts.

"Oh, Bryn," he groaned as he grew closer to climax. Bryn pushed her hand's hard into the table, pushing herself back, moving her hips in rhythm to match Erik's. They moaned each other's names as they both exploded in ecstasy.

The sounds of their panting breaths were the only sound in the hut as Erik scooped Bryn in his arms and carried her to his bed. He curled himself around her, and she sank into him. Two warriors lost in passion.

Erik looked longingly into Bryn's eyes. She stared back, bringing a hand to his cheek; she was feeling things for Erik she never expected but was unsure of what future they could have. He was preparing for war and planned for future glory. She was a Runemaster, a warrior no longer fit for battle.

As the thoughts crossed her mind, her thoughts went back to the conversations of the evening, and the idea bothered her. She needed to cast to try and get answers one last time.

Bryn waited for Erik to drift off to sleep, waiting for the sound of his soft snoring to prove he was in a deep sleep before she dressed and headed back to her tent.

On arrival at her tent, she freshened up and prepared to cast. She collected her runes and brought the questions she needed to answer to the forefront of her mind. She threw the rune stone tiles across the table, but before she could search for answers, a group of men burst into her tent.

She looked up, anger flooding her face at the intrusion. She was outnumbered; it was the Jarl's men. She reached for her staff, but before she could fight back, she was bound, gagged, and dragged out of her tent and away into the night.

CHAPTER 8

ERIK AWOKE when he could no longer feel Bryn's presence next to him. A sudden feeling of hurt and longing descended over him. He realised he needed her; he would not likely find a woman like her again. Someone who shared a love for battle fought to prove themselves in a world that often cast them aside.

He freshened and dressed, taking extra care to look his best. He didn't know what he would say to her, but he knew he had to try and fight for her affection.

He arrived at her tent and immediately knew something was wrong. He burst inside and found the space trashed. The table overturned, her runes were scattered on the floor, and the large stone tablet she had carved only days before was smashed. *What in the name of Asgärd,* he thought, anger and worry taking hold of his heart. He ran outside, and as he rose over the hills; he noticed the tracks in the dirt. She had been taken, he realised, taking off at great speed and following the tracks.

Erik charged through the settlement, following the tracks towards the dock. He looked ahead and saw a sight that brought both joy and fear to his heart.

Bryn was surrounded by five of the Jarl's men, but she wasn't an ordinary helpless maiden. His Bryn was a fearsome warrior, and she showed that with force.

Erik ran towards the scene as Bryn punched and kicked her way free. Bryn brought her knee to the groin of the biggest guard and cracked her head against his nose. As he grabbed his face and cried out in pain, she pulled the sword from his hilt and swung, slicing another guard clean across the stomach, and spilling his guts on the floor. Despite her injured leg, she fought bravely, taking down two more of the Jarl's men before Erik saw her stance waver.

The guard brought down his axe, forcing Bryn to stagger against the force as it clashed with her sword. She needed Erik, and he would not allow her to be hurt, not when he could do something to stop it. Charging forward, he grabbed the guard around the waist and flung him off the dock, making him crash into the water.

Erik helped Bryn to her feet. She smiled at him. They continued to fight, but it wasn't long before they were outnumbered as more of the Jarl's men joined the fight.

Bryn and Erik stood back-to-back, their weapons outstretched, ready to attack when more men surrounded; a mix of axes, swords, and arrows aimed steadily at them.

Left with no choice, they lowered their weapons and were swiftly led the rest of the way to the ship where the Jarl was waiting for them.

CHAPTER 9

As THE JARL'S men dragged Bryn and Erik onto the ship, Erik scanned for a way to escape. He glanced over to check on Bryn to see that she was doing the same. Soldiers filled the vessel, in every corner there were armed guards. Each man stood ready to attack at the first sign of trouble.

The guards roughly dragged and pushed the pair aboard the vessel and down into the Jarl's private quarters, where Bryn was tossed at Halfden's feet. As Bryn fell to the floor, two more guards grabbed Erik; they needed the extra manpower to accommodate his size.

"Well, well, well. What do we have here? I asked for the Runemaster, and I also got a second son. To what do I owe the pleasure?" The Jarl sneered as he picked Bryn up by her hair.

Bryn didn't take to being manhandled in such a way and lashed out her fist, connecting with the Jarl's jaw.

The Jarl tossed her into the waiting arms of two of his guards and slapped her across the face with the back of his hand, the ring on his middle finger slicing open her lip.

Erik tried to launch forward to attack the Jarl, but he was held back; he noticed how they struggled, the four men restraining him. *One strong, swift movement and I would be free*, he thought.

"He attacked trying to free her, Sire; we had no choice but to bring him too," one of the guards answered.

The Jarl waved off the man's answer, turning his attention back to Bryn. "You have proven to be a thorn in my side. I have heard of your readings: years of hard work almost destroyed by your meddling." An evil grin spread across his lips. "But you won't be meddling into anyone else's business much longer."

"Do with me what you will. Everyone knows about your scheming with the Celts and Lord Beecham. Sooner or later, the King will know too. My work is done," Bryn snarled, spitting in the Jarl's face.

Erik's face twitched into a smile. The more he saw the real Bryn, the more he was determined they were meant to be together.

"You can kill us all you want; my brothers know of your theft and treason. Wait until the King's suspicions are confirmed. What will he do with you when he finds out you have been taking the Danegeld for yourself?" Erik barked, pulling against his restraints, checking for weaknesses in their grasp.

The Jarl turned to Erik and laughed, "You think this is about the Danegeld? But, of course, being a second son, I suppose you could not be expected to understand what's at stake."

He laughed, turning to Bryn. "What do you see in him, a respected warrior turned Runemaster like yourself? You can do so much better than a pitiful second son."

The Jarl sneered, stroking Bryn's face and shooting Erik a knowing, evil look.

Erik and Bryn shared a glance; if this wasn't about Danegeld, what was it about? What if Bryn had read the rules wrong? The Jarl's words only raised more questions. The Jarl watched the pair intently before bursting out into laughter once more.

"You have no clue, do you? This is glorious, fighting and dying for a cause in which you know nothing!" he bellowed. "Men, prepare a vessel for these two, bind them, and toss them aboard!"

"What do you plan on doing with us?" Bryn demanded, struggling to free herself.

The Jarl was no longer entertained by the pair and was rolling his eyes. "You two will be seen leaving together, a tryst, running away together? It matters not… and while your brothers watch you sail into the distance, they will watch you burn."

The Jarl smirked at Erik. "Oh, and if he tries to resist...." The Jarl pulled a blade from his boot and handed it to one of the men restraining Bryn, "Slit her throat."

Erik's face blanched as his eyes darted to the blade now being held to Bryn's throat.

The thought of her being hurt due to his actions had him rethinking every move he had calculated in his head. He knew Bryn would not appreciate his attempts to save her, but at that moment, he didn't care if, by doing nothing, she would be unharmed. He would do just that. Nothing.

Bound and placed in a small craft, Erik and Bryn were pushed out to sea, taken further away from shore with the tide.

"Can you free yourself?" Bryn asked as she struggled to wriggle out of the rope that cut into her wrist. Erik shook his head as he, too, pulled at his binds.

Bryn looked back towards the dock at the archers waiting for their command.

"You could have taken down all those men; you could have freed us both," she snarled, sucking air in through gritted teeth as the rope chafed her wrists.

Erik looked up at her, a look in his eyes she didn't expect to see. "They had a knife to your throat; if I had tried, they would have killed you."

"I can take care of myself," she answered.

Erik looked up at her and smiled. "I don't doubt that for a second. If these are my last moments, I'm proud to say I had the honour to fight alongside you."

He said it with great sincerity. Bryn felt a warmth spread through her, swiftly followed by sorrow as she watched the archers light their arrows. "I'm sorry. I've spent my life since my injury fighting to prove myself to the world. I'm often looked at like a useless cripple; you have not once treated me as such, and all I have done is fight you at every turn. It's a hard habit to break."

She watched the archers draw their bows, waiting for the second they would loose their arrows and death would come flying towards them.

"At least we had last night; I would not like to meet death not knowing what it felt like to feel you rise," she smirked, proud of her joke.

Erik smirked back at her and chuckled when she bowed her head, and her cheeks blushed red. "Death will not greet us tonight, my Bryn. Not while I still draw breath."

Grunts and metal clashing from the docks broke them out of their moment; they both looked back to see Abjörn, Sören, and Ryker fighting the Jarl's men.

Dittmer and a few men mounted a craft and sailed speedily towards their boat.

Once Dittmer had freed his brother and Bryn and helped them back ashore, they too joined the fight. Erik made an effort to stay close to Bryn in case her leg gave out again, but from the men she brought down, he was proud to see she didn't need his help.

Their group was outnumbered four to one, but the greater numbers were no match against the Jürgensen brothers' size and ferocious fighting skills.

"The Jarl!" yelled one of the other fighters, pointing to the Jarl who hid behind a small group of his men.

"Coward!" yelled Bryn as she hobbled over to a fallen archer and snatched up his bow.

Erik saw her plan and charged towards the Jarl, slicing a sword through every man that got in his path.

Bryn fired arrow after arrow, landing each shot square in the chest, swiftly bringing down the Jarl's guard.

Abjörn followed his brother while Ryker, Dittmer, and Sören tore through the men on The Jarl's ship.

Arrows, alight with flame, flew through the air aiming at the settlement. It was a distraction tactic to try and split the forces. Firtha, Sima, and the other women who were not tending to the children quickly extinguished the flames.

At the sight of their wives in danger, Sören and Abjörn flared with anger, burying their axes deep into every man in their path.

"Bryn, the archers!" Dittmer yelled, and Bryn turned and brought the archers on the ship down. She dropped her bow and grabbed a large axe from a fallen soldier nearby; she lifted it high over her head and sent it flying through the air. It connected between the shoulder blades of a fighter approaching Erik from behind.

Erik spun to see Bryn fighting and noticed her leg give out once more.

"Abjörn, the Jarl before he gets away!" Erik bellowed, making a swift turn, and heading towards Bryn. He hit the man with his axe and sent him flying backwards before grabbing Bryn around her waist and helping her to her feet.

"I don't need your help," she insisted, pulling a small blade she had locked away in her waistband and throwing it with precision into the eye of a nearby fighter.

"Tough, you are getting it whether you like it or not," Erik snapped, holding tighter onto her.

"You can still fight with my help; now stop complaining!" Erik barked, slicing his sword through the air.

CHAPTER 10

THE BROTHERS ASSESSED the damage after the battle. They had taken a few losses as they gathered the bodies of their fallen men. But somehow, the Jarl had managed to escape.

"He can't have got far; he won't have many men with him. We could still catch him," Sören said as he wiped the blood from his axe.

"We don't have time to waste searching for him," Abjörn said, rubbing his hand over his face.

Sima, Abjörn's wife, stepped forward. "We know he has a history with my father; who is to say he won't have gone to him? He has nowhere else to turn to that makes sense."

Bryn propped herself upon a wooden post. "Sima is correct; the Jarl said something to Erik and me when he held us captive. I think there is more than meets the eye here." She turned to Erik. "I must consult the runes; I need to cast. What if I missed something before?"

Erik agreed, and they all followed to Bryn's tent. She gathered her scattered tiles off the floor as Dittmer and Sören fixed the table to an upright position.

Bryn grabbed her tiles in hand and held them tight to her chest as she closed her eyes and brought her questions to the forefront of her mind. Then, she let out a slow, calming breath and cast the runes.

She looked over the tiles and fell silent; the answers she sought were not in England. She looked up at the group; the brothers and their wives all stood waiting anxiously for her answers.

"What is it, Bryn?" Erik asked with concern in his voice at the look in her eyes.

"The runes, they speak," she began, looking back at the stones once more. "I see separation in our futures. Not all the answers lie here on these shores. Some must stay, and some must sail back home to Denmark. We must speak to the King while the rest pursue the Jarl. That is the only solution if our questions are to be answered."

She fell quiet, looking over the runes again and again. For the first time in the longest time, she felt she was part of something bigger than herself. Erik and his brothers accepted her for the warrior that she was and never judged her as a cripple. They fought with her in battle, and now the family she had joined was being forced apart. The thought broke her heart, but she knew this was bigger than all of them.

A plan was set, goodbyes were said, and embraces remembered.

"It is settled then," Erik said, looking around the room as everyone nodded their agreement. They left Bryn's tent, taking the next steps towards their needed answers. The group was sad as they parted ways.

EPILOGUE

THE BROTHERS PREPARED A SHIP; its passengers being Abjörn and his wife, Sima, and Bryn and Erik.

It was agreed that Abjörn, the eldest representative of the family, would speak with the King. Bryn decided it was best to testify as the Runemaster to what her father sent and what she had witnessed regarding the Jarl.

Erik was not prepared to leave Bryn, so he insisted on travelling to Denmark. It was going to be a long journey from England to Denmark. Erik planned on using that time to get to know Bryn very intimately and repeatedly along their journey.

"Why are you looking at me like that?" Bryn smiled as Erik eyed her like she was a delicious treat.

"You are something else, Bryn the Runemaster. I have never looked to a woman before except for a night of passion. Yet the thought of another night without you at my side stabs at my heart."

He stepped closer and loomed over her, running his hand through her hair and caressing her cheek. "We are the same, you and I - both fighting to prove ourselves in a world ready to reject us. I can't think of anyone else in the world I would want to fight that battle with than you."

He brought his lips down to meet hers. Erik gently led Bryn back towards the cot in the corner. Bryn smiled as she pushed him backwards, causing him to fall. He smiled, slowly undressing as Bryn removed her clothes.

Erik slid to the edge of the bed and ran his hand up her mangled leg, trailing kisses from her knee to her thigh. Bryn looked down at him and smiled before pushing him back and climbing astride of him.

Slowly she lowered herself onto his shaft, gasping as he filled every inch of her. She sat savouring every inch of his deliciousness before she found her rhythm. Erik gripped her hips, enjoying the pace she set; he moaned her name as she clenched herself around him.

Erik ran his hands up her torso to cup her breasts as she placed her hands on his hard chest of muscle to steady herself. They moaned each other's names as the pleasure built between them. Bryn began to slow as her leg twinged with pain. Noticing the twinge in her eyes, Erik sat up straight, gripping her hair in his hands and kissing her passionately before wrapping his arms around her and flipping positions.

He loved the sight of her underneath him as he placed her good leg on his shoulder, stretching her wide. Erik slowly slid himself back inside and shivered at the gloriousness that was Bryn. He increased his pace as the pair drew closer and closer to claiming their ecstasy.

"Erik!" Bryn cried as her pleasure took over her, forcing her to arch her back as her body filled with fire.

"Bryn!" Erik bellowed as he stilled, filling her with his pleasure. They fell around each other, and Erik pulled Bryn into his arms as he kissed her gently on her forehead.

"I think I am going to enjoy our trip back home," Bryn smiled, running her fingers through the sweaty mass of hair on Erik's chest.

THE END

RYKER

BESTED BY THE VALKYRIE

PROLOGUE

RYKER AND DITTMER SAT WAITING, perturbed by the events since Abjörn and Erik had left for Denmark. The two brothers were frustrated. They loved battle, especially when defending something they both held so close to their hearts. Their family, country, and, of course, seeking revenge for their father.

Sören had sent out patrols, guarding against any attacks he thought might result from the Jarl's escape. So far, the patrols had reported nothing noteworthy. To Ryker's way of thinking, Sören had proven to be no fun at all. When Abjörn and Erik announced they were travelling back to Denmark and leaving Sören in charge, Dittmer and Ryker had been inwardly pleased. Sören's hot head would result in tales of glory for their brothers' return. So far, the closest thing they had to report was the news of Sören and Firtha expecting. While they were happy for their brother and his wife, they felt Sören had grown soft and overly cautious now that he was in charge.

Ryker polished the blade of his axe while Dittmer ran a stone along the edge of his sword. It had been a while since their weapons had tasted blood, and they wanted their weapons to be ready for the next attack. Sören approached, looking far too relaxed for the brothers' liking. It vexed them both, though neither spoke of it to the other.

"News on the patrols? I haven't had a report from you in days,"

Sören said, ignoring the daggers both his younger siblings shot from their eyes.

"There is nothing to report, just like there wasn't three days ago, or three days before that," Ryker said, admiring his handiwork with his axe.

"If you allow us to search for the Jarl or even confront Lord Beecham, then maybe we would have something to report," Dittmer said, not looking up from his blade. Ryker well knew how much Dittmer was trying to control his temper. His grim expression told Ryker that his younger brother was very annoyed with Sören.

"We have been through this, Dittmer. The best thing to do is have patience. What good is there in starting a war when our numbers are depleted? The best thing for us to do is wait for Abjörn and Erik's return," Sören said. But his voice betrayed him. He didn't believe a word of what he spoke. He was just concerned with leaving Firtha alone and what might happen to her and the babe should he fall in battle.

Dittmer shot to his feet and stomped over to his brother, standing so close they practically touched noses. Ryker could feel the anger rolling off Dittmer like heat on a summer's day.

"If we sit and do nothing, we are giving Beecham and the Jarl more time to build their forces. They will think we are weak and afraid. Are you afraid, brother?" Dittmer growled, challenging Sören.

Ryker stood, bracing himself for carnage if his siblings decided to fight.

"I am afraid of nothing," Sören growled back through his teeth. Things were headed to dangerous territory.

"Yet, you have us sitting here like lambs awaiting slaughter," Dittmer spat back. He would not be intimidated by his older brother, too pig-headed to back down.

"This is why I was left in charge. You would allow your temper to cloud your judgement. Your hot head would get us into more trouble. So we sit and wait. That's an order!" Sören barked as he turned to leave.

Dittmer uttered an insult under his breath, too quiet for Ryker to hear correctly, but Sören was closer than Ryker was. Whatever insult or slur had been spoken proved to be the spark needed for the brothers to ignite. Sören instantly turned and ran at his brother, grabbing him by his collar.

"What did you say?" Sören yelled.

Dittmer smirked, shoving his brother backwards, quickly freeing himself from his grasp. "I said, maybe we should check between your legs because clearly, your wife has bigger balls than you," Dittmer replied.

Ryker took half a step forward, wondering if he needed to intercede. Sören's eyes blazed with fury. He needed to separate his brothers before things got out of hand. Jumping in front of the two, he ducked just dodging Sören's fist as it flew through the air.

"Enough brothers, we have more important things to focus our energy on rather than fighting amongst ourselves," Ryker insisted, doing his best to defuse the situation. Sören huffed and stormed away. Dittmer stood with a look of pride on his face, feeling he had won that round.

"Sören has a need to be cautious. Firtha is with child. Besides, Abjörn would not have left him in charge if he didn't trust his judgement," Ryker said, trying to make his brother see sense. Dittmer growled in frustration, unwilling to admit that Ryker had a point. In the end, he too stormed off, only in the other direction.

Ryker watched his brothers depart in opposing directions, each blazing with frustration and anger. Sören would be well enough. It was the youngest brother who worried him. Ryker thought Dittmer needed to lighten up. He had been strung as tight as a bow for the longest time. *He needs to laugh, to have fun and let off some steam*, Ryker thought.

Just then, an idea popped into his head. With a smile, Ryker turned and left his post.

CHAPTER 1

ASTRID WIPED HER BROW. She grew tired of all her chores. It was the height of summer, and the sun was scorching hot. Thankfully, she hadn't travelled far from the Swordswomen's cottage just outside the settlement. After collecting and chopping wood, she ventured past the trees to hunt for new berries and other edible treats.

She hadn't travelled through the forest this way before and was delighted when she stumbled across a stream. Sweat soaked her, and the water looked refreshing and inviting as it trickled down the hill. Her water pouch had run dry earlier, and she was parched. Scooping a handful of water, she knelt down to drink. The water was as delightfully cool as it looked, which gave her an idea.

I've finished all my chores for the day. A quick dip wouldn't hurt, she thought. It was a wicked thought, but the water was far too inviting to pass by. Placing her bucket of berries near a bush, she glanced around, making sure eyes were not watching. Then, happy to note that the coast was clear, she untied her outer dress, draping it over a bush. It was best to leave her cotton shift on. After all, someone might still pass by.

Stepping into the water, she sighed with pleasure as the water cooled and soothed her burning skin. Sinking deeper, she swam from one side of the stream to the other and back, enjoying the water stroking her skin. She dropped her head back, allowing the cool water to soak her hair, and shivered as the water worked its way through her hair, all the way down to her scalp, tickling her enough to give her a case of the shivers. Fully refreshed, she headed back towards her belongings. Here she settled on a rock just beneath the surface of the water, resting her arms in the soft grass of the bank, closing her eyes and tilting her head back, letting the sun bathe her face.

A smile spread across her face as she sat, enjoying the water and the sounds of nature. Birds sang in the trees, and the leaves rustled as the summer breeze passed through the trees. All was as it should be.

A branch snapping underfoot brought Astrid back to her senses. Her eyes snapped open, and she stilled. She wasn't alone. Listening carefully, she tracked the location of the noise. It came from the direction of her things, just over her right shoulder. Sitting upright, she looked over in time to see a tall Viking warrior dressed ready for battle standing by the bush, her dress in his hands.

The Viking stood looking down at Astrid, stunned. Judging from his red face, he seemed embarrassed to be caught stealing her dress. Astrid sat unafraid, being a swordswoman herself. She didn't doubt she could knock him on his backside.

"I don't think it's your size," she smirked as she slowly stepped back onto the bank, water flowing off her. She was very aware of how her shift had become transparent and planned on using that to her advantage. In Astrid's experience, most males didn't know how to handle a strong woman. She was sure this one would prove no different.

His eyes travelled the length of her as she slowly took a step closer to him.

"I have heard of men like you, those who prefer the company of other men and like to wear dresses," she said, eying him up and down. "I have to say, I never would have pegged you for being inclined in such a way," she teased, keeping a close eye on the axe at his hip and the blade tucked into his boot. Astrid couldn't help but notice how striking he was, tall and muscular, with a strong jaw and dark eyes she could easily get lost in. He would have been quite handsome if he weren't standing slack-jawed, unable to speak.

"Are you a mute too? I hold no hope for the people you fight for if the mere sight of me has struck you dumb," she said, finally stepping close enough to him to snatch her dress from his grasp.

His scent filled her nose, and she couldn't help but notice how her nipples had reacted to him, standing in stiff peaks beneath the wet cotton of her clothing.

She liked how he looked her over. She was not self-conscious in the least. She was a strong, slender woman and almost matched him in height. She had always known the effects of her beauty on the opposite sex. It was one of the reasons she had become a sword maiden. She'd wanted to be known for other things rather than just her beauty.

It was time this stranger learned these things about her.

She snatched the dress from his hands, rolling her eyes at the Viking's stupidity. He was young, but he could obviously fight and handle himself well by his size and build. "Stupid boy, I could have easily pulled that axe from your side and buried it in your skull in the time you have been gawping at me. What is wrong with you?" she snapped, holding the dress close to her chest covering herself from his prying eyes.

The Viking began to stutter, unable to form a complete sentence. "It was all in jest, I...Dittmer...not," he stammered, looking over her, shaken to his core.

"Speak. Are you a man or a boy? Speak clearly," Astrid demanded, ignoring her soaking wet shift and stepping back into her dress while she waited for his reply.

"I do not wear dresses. I didn't know it belonged to anyone. I was planning on using it to get my brother in trouble. It was meant in jest, just in jest," he stuttered, still thrown by the beauty standing in front of him with her hands on her hips, annoyance painted on her face.

CHAPTER 2

ASTRID EYED THE VIKING SUSPICIOUSLY. She had never heard anything so foolish. How could taking her dress be a jest on his brother? *Perhaps he is tricking me? Trying to make me look ridiculous?* Astrid frowned. She did not like people trying to make fun of her or make her look foolish. The more she thought about it, the more she grew irritated. She began to circle the young Viking, sizing him up.

"Dittmer? Is that your name?" she asked, enjoying him squirming under her gaze.

He took a step back away from her, and Astrid noted how he drew closer to the stream.

"No, Dittmer is my brother. I am Ryker," he responded, taking another step back as she glared him down. Her presence appeared to unsettle him.

"Ryker? You are a Jürgensen brother?" she asked.

He nodded vigorously, still stuttering as he fought to answer her.

"Embarrassing, your lineage is famous for being ferocious and fearless, yet here you are made helpless as the mere sight of a woman," she spat. Ryker was now close enough to the stream for Astrid to fulfil her plan.

"Helpless? I am scarcely—"

"Boo," she yelled as she pushed him off the bank.

Startled, he grabbed at her to stop his fall. Instead, he dragged her down with him. The two tumbled into the stream, with Astrid winding up sprawled across his rock-hard chest. She looked down into his dreamy brown eyes.

He smirked back at her. "Why hello there," he said, laughing to himself at the alarm and irritation upon her face. Astrid placed her palms flat upon his chest that she might push herself up, not noticing she was straddling him. She couldn't help but see how nice his chest felt under her hands.

Nice? What was wrong with her?

"Idiot, why did you do that?" she snapped, swatting his chest but not making an attempt to move. She liked the feel of him beneath her, and she had to admit the view was pleasing to the eye.

Ryker splashed a handful of water into her face. The act caught her by surprise, and Astrid shrieked in shock. Now it was her turn to gape slack-jawed at him.

"Relax, you can't say you are not having fun. Besides, I quite like the view of you on top of me," Ryker chuckled, splashing her again.

Astrid grew increasingly vexed by his childish behaviour and smacked him in the chest once more, attempting to stand. But as she rose to her feet, Ryker swiped his leg under hers, making her fall backwards into the water. Astrid splashed down hard, momentarily losing her breath at the force of her back hitting the water.

Before Astrid could make a move to stand, Ryker swam over to her, splashing her again. She coughed as water entered her lungs. She splashed him back as she regained her breath.

"I think I much preferred you in your underdress," Ryker said, his voice a deep growl, treading water near her.

"Get away from me, you big oaf," she said, and she couldn't help but let out a small chuckle as she splashed him back. Ryker tore off his armour and tunic, tossing them with force over to the bank, allowing them to dry in the heat of the sun. Astrid stood admiring the wall of muscle standing before her.

"It's only fair, tit for tat as it were," he said with a wink.

Astrid felt heat blossom in her cheeks. She shrieked as Ryker swam over, scooping her up in his arms. He held her tightly to him, her bosom pushed up, almost rubbing against his short, neat beard. Astrid steadied herself by placing her hands on his chest. She smiled at him as she let her fingers trace the hard muscle there for the second time.

Oh yes, she liked touching him.

"I will admit, for someone who acts like a child, you definitely have the physique of a man," she said, her voice breathy as the heat between them intensified. Ryker smiled and tossed her backwards, causing her to splash back down into the water. When she came up for air, wiping her eyes, Ryker was doubled over laughing hard. "You should see your face!" he bellowed.

Annoyed but enjoying the fun, Astrid swam over, pushing him under the water and splashing him several times as he came up for air. "How do you like that?" she laughed.

They continued to frolic, acting like babes, enjoying the cool water in the hot summer sun, and despite their first encounter, enjoying each other's company. At least they were until reality came crashing down around them.

Another strong, tall Viking came storming through the trees. This man bears a striking resemblance to Ryker. Astrid knew instantly this had to be his younger brother Dittmer.

"What goes on here? Is everything all right? I heard screaming..." he began, stopping when he noticed the two wrapped in an embrace. "Oh, I see," he said with a smirk, backing away slowly. "I will leave you two lovers, be." He winked at Ryker and turned to go.

Astrid was appalled at the accusation. She swatted Ryker hard on the shoulder and pushed herself away from him, wading through the water to the bank.

"It is not what you think. He is not my lover," Astrid protested, dragging her skirts behind her as she stepped onto the bank. She looked back, expecting Ryker to explain, but instead, he burst out laughing once more. Astrid's mind flooded with annoyance. She was not a joke and didn't like being treated like one. She looked over to Dittmer, who was holding back a chuckle himself. She could see his laughter all over his face as he tried to force away a smile.

"You two are children, both of you. Instead of standing shooting accusations at me, stealing dresses, and acting like fools, why not do something useful?" she snapped, storming over and grabbing her bucket of berries. "You are Jürgensens. Live up to your family name! While you frolic around, the Jarl's men go free. Make yourself useful and go after them!" she yelled and stormed off towards home.

CHAPTER 3

RYKER AWOKE the next day feeling guilty. He had not meant to insult or upset the young woman. Worse, the more he thought about it, the more her words haunted him. *Live up to your family name.* After he broke his fast and dressed, he headed out through the woods past the settlement, hunting for her cottage. He saw her outside grabbing wood from the woodpile before heading back indoors. Taking a moment to collect himself and think of what to say, he walked up to the door, knocking louder than he intended. She swung the door open impatiently. When her eyes fell on him, her brow furrowed, and her features hardened.

"What do you want?" she demanded.

"I came here to apologise for my behaviour yesterday," he said simply.

She looked him over unimpressed. "I'm not interested," she said, moving to close the door, but Ryker shot out a hand and held the door open.

"Please, may I come inside?" he asked as gently as he could.

She refused to move. "State your business here and leave me alone," she answered, folding her arms, waiting him out.

Ryker stood, not knowing what to do. He'd hoped she would just move aside. But she stood looking blankly at him. He rubbed his hand over his face nervously.

"I'm sorry, I was trying to get my brother to relax and thought a play in jest would do the trick. I didn't mean to get you involved. I certainly didn't mean to make you feel foolish," he said.

The maiden stood unflinching. From the look on her face, she was expecting more. She shifted, crossing and uncrossing her arms.

"I shouldn't have dragged you in the river with me. I lost myself in the moment. I can be childish at times. I didn't even get a chance to ask your name," he said, hoping she would tell him. He hadn't been able to shake the image of her as she stepped from the river in clothing so wet that he'd been able to clearly see every last inch of her.

"And?" she asked, and as if he read her thoughts, he knew what she wanted to hear.

"I'm sorry for ogling you when you were.... when you..." he stuttered again, feeling his face growing hotter by the minute.

Why am I blushing like a woman? What is wrong with me?

"Astrid, my name is Astrid," she answered, rolling her eyes and gesturing for him to enter the house. She stepped aside and opened the door wider. Ryker smiled and thanked her as he ducked to step inside. Thankfully, the door frame was the lowest part of the building. He was happy to draw himself up to his full height again inside without banging his head on the wooden beams supporting the roof.

The cottage was quiet, with no one else there. A fireplace with a small black pot hanging ready for use near the back wall. On one side of the cottage was a small table with two chairs, and her bed was on the other side. The part that grabbed his attention the most was the pile of armour and weapons beside her bed. It made her that much more intriguing.

"You are a warrior?" he asked, walking over, and picking up her sword. It was an impressive piece, and the weight surprised him.

Astrid stalked over, snatching the blade and tossing it onto her bed.

"Yes, I came here on the second ship to fight with the other swordswomen. But since I made this place my home, there has been no action to speak of. I spend most of my time now supplementing the settlement's supplies. It keeps me busy," she answered as she walked out the door at the back next to the fireplace. "I have work to do."

Ryker followed her into a small, fenced-off garden and sat on a dead tree stump where he could watch as she turned the sizeable top stone of a quern, grinding grain and making flour.

"I would like to see you in battle. Your sword is rather impressive, and I can tell that you are a strong woman," he said, pulling down his tunic to show a bruise on his collar bone. "A reminder of our first encounter, I shall cherish it," he joked, clutching his hands to his heart and fluttering his eyes, mimicking a love-struck maiden.

"Continue down this path, and I shall give you a few more," she said, gathering the flour she had made and heading back inside. She placed the flour on the table and headed to a barrel filled with water. Using a small bowl, she scooped some up and took a sip.

Ryker shifted, suddenly uncomfortable as he watched a drop sliding down her lips and chin, gently falling to her breast. He moved quickly, hoping she wouldn't notice him enjoying the view as she wiped the water from her bosom.

"What did you do back home?" Ryker asked, pulling out a chair and sitting down, ignoring the creaking of the wood as it complained under his weight.

"I worked on my father's farm. It wasn't a bad life. But as I grew older, I realised it wasn't my strength or mind that drew me notice from those around me; it was my looks. I decided that wasn't good enough. I am just as strong and capable as any man. So, I trained as a sword maiden, and after having some success in battle, I decided I wanted more. When the ships were readied to come to this settlement, I was first in line to volunteer," she said, offering him some water.

It was just as hot as the day before, so Ryker accepted the refreshing drink gladly. He thought a moment while he slaked his thirst. Honesty called for honesty.

"I will tell you something now that must not leave this room. I have been jealous of my brothers—the ones who have found themselves women. Firtha, Sima, and Bryn are all strong, fierce women. Unfortunately, many of the women I encounter have no love for battle. So, I'm glad I had the chance to meet you." He spoke from the heart, for once not kidding around.

Astrid, taken back by his comments, offered a subject change. She wanted to talk about the battle. She wanted to find out when her sword would next taste blood and when she would gain honour.

"Why have you and your brothers done nothing since the incident with the Jarl? What are you waiting for?" she asked directly, sitting opposite him, determined to get answers. Ryker was shocked by her directness and hated that he didn't have an answer. However, it was not up to him to take action. Abjörn had left Sören in command, and he told her as much.

"Believe me, I, like yourself, crave action, but it is not my decision. Sören is in command, and he thinks we should wait. He believes war is unnecessary until my brothers return from Denmark," He shook his head, his lip curling in disgust. "The Jarl has not attacked. Neither has Lord Beecham," he finished with a shrug, not knowing what else he could tell her.

"Well, I think the time to attack is now. No man, woman, or child in the neighbouring villages would help Beecham after all he has done," she said. She rose to fetch a bucket of vegetables she had collected that morning. She dropped the bucket on the table and pulled the branches and leaves apart. Then, she pulled a blade from her boot and began to chop the vegetables, tossing the freshly cut pieces into a bowl she pulled from a shelf.

Ryker was confused by her words. Did she know something he didn't? How had she come across such information? His interest was piqued. This could be his chance to change Sören's mind. and his pulse raced with excitement.

"What do you mean?" he asked, leaning closer.

Astrid looked back, confused. "What?"

"How do you know that they wouldn't help?" he persisted, flirtation was forgotten for the moment.

"I hear things," she said simply.

Not satisfied with her answer, Ryker pushed for more.

"I've been trading with the Scots village over the hill since I have been tending to livestock. I had the need to trade for the goods I was lacking," she began slicing her knife through a carrot. "Beecham's been taking from his people. They have less food, and less coin. Especially of late. They are worse off than ever."

Astrid's attention had been so focused on preparing vegetables for dinner that evening that she hadn't noticed Ryker fall silent. She finally looked up to see Ryker staring blankly, a look on his face as if she had slapped him herself.

"What?" she asked as she began to grow worried. Ryker jumped to his feet, taking her hand so suddenly he knocked her bowl of vegetables onto the floor. "Come with me. This is vital information. It would help if you told Sören what you know," he insisted, dragging her out the door, with utter disregard to her protests of annoyance.

CHAPTER 4

DITTMER STOOD ARMS FOLDED, not believing the story Astrid and Ryker had just told. He had had enough of his brother's fun and games. They were at war. This was no time to be fooling around.

"Come on, brother, this is exactly the information we need to get Sören to change his mind. Do you not long for battle? To get revenge for father?" Ryker pleaded.

Unfortunately, Ryker's antics had led his brother to think his words unbelievable.

"Get serious for once in your life, brother! You know that is exactly what I want. But how am I to believe you? Yesterday I found you two fooling around in the stream. Today, you come at me with some crazy story about villagers. How is this information even helpful?" Dittmer asked. He looked over at Astrid with anger. Dittmer clearly thought all his brothers had grown soft since they met their women. And this was just another prime example of how he was right.

Sören gazed at his wife Firtha and smiled. He knew the effect women could have on a warrior's mind. Glancing over at the pair, he noticed how they shared a look that could only mean one thing. Attraction.

"Dittmer is right. What does this prove? He is taking from his own rather than us. I don't see how this is relevant," Sören said. He crossed the room to retrieve some water, and while his back was turned, Astrid looked over to Firtha, pleading with her eyes for help.

"Maybe I can find out something. You know how these people once turned to me for spells and positions. They will trust me and speak the truth," she said, winking at Astrid. Of course, Firth knew her husband wouldn't allow her to make such a journey, not while she was so close to birthing their child. Astrid looked at her with new respect. Firtha was craftier than she'd initially supposed.

Predictably, Sören reacted just how his wife thought he would. He turned, facing them with fury in his eyes. "No, not a chance. You are not getting involved in this. You could give birth any moment now. Do you want to make a journey like that over something that could prove to be nothing? No, I will not allow it. You need to stay here and rest," Sören yelled.

It was evident to everyone just how concerned he was for his child's birth and how nervous he was about his impending fatherhood. Every move he made was extra cautious. Even a shadow seemed to put him on edge. Astrid found it charming, while his brothers found it annoying, from the look on their faces. Finally, after a moment of pacing and shooting angry looks over to his wife, who sat with amusement on her face, Sören stopped.

"Astrid, you know these villagers. You go. You have a relationship with them. They will talk to you. Find out as much as you can. Ryker will accompany you for protection," Sören insisted as he embraced his wife, stroking her rounded belly lovingly.

"Astrid doesn't need much protecting; she has a mean right hook," Ryker mumbled with a smirk on his face.

Astrid gave his ankle a swift kick. "Behave yourself, fool," she murmured. While his words rang true, now was not a time for joking. Sören and Dittmer already found an issue with her information. If they saw Ryker joking around, they would likely call off the mission.

Astrid was filled with pride, and she had waited for a moment to prove herself. If battle approached, she was all for it. She nodded her acceptance of the mission to Sören and mouthed a silent, 'thank you' to Firtha, who gave her a knowing wink. As she turned to leave, she noticed Dittmer eyeing her suspiciously. Dittmer was going to be harder to win over than she thought.

CHAPTER 5

RYKER AND ASTRID passed the settlement gate on their horses, riding west towards the hills.

"I'm glad we get to do this mission together," Ryker said, smiling over at Astrid. She blushed and smiled back. She had noticed that she was instantly attracted to Ryker. She found his childlike nature charming. And she liked that he brought out a more relaxed, almost innocent part of her that she hadn't even known was there. She had spent so many years being so serious in her mission to become a sword maiden that she felt she had forgotten how to have fun. She may have been annoyed the day before when he pulled her into the stream. Still, she had to admit, in the moments before Dittmer came and interrupted their fun, she had been enjoying herself.

"Hold up, I'm coming with you," Dittmer yelled after them. They glanced over their shoulders to see him on his horse galloping towards them. Astrid and Ryker shared a look of dismay. *Dittmer here to spoil our fun again*, Astrid thought.

"Why are you here, brother?" Ryker asked, unable to hide the annoyance in his voice.

"I am here to keep you two on course," he answered simply, pushing his horse between both of theirs, forcing them to move apart.

"So, you are here to supervise? Correct me if I'm wrong, brother, but are you not the youngest of us all?" Ryker smirked.

"Yet I am more mature than your foolish backside," Dittmer shot back.

She couldn't help it. Astrid let out a quiet chuckle.

They rode for a mile in silence while Ryker frowned, trying to think up a way to get Dittmer to leave them alone. Suddenly, an idea came to him. If he could direct the line of conversation, he could drop a little white lie that might fool Dittmer enough to give him and Astrid some space.

"So, Astrid, what is the plan? This is your mission; Dittmer and I will follow your lead. Right, brother?" Ryker asked.

Dittmer flashed him a look before nodding his agreement.

"When we arrive, try not to look intimidating. The best place to start is the farm. They hold the biggest grudge against Beecham," Astrid answered, looking off into the distance as if she could already see their destination.

"And we are headed to the Scots village?" Ryker asked.

Astrid shot him a look of confusion. How could he not know where they were going when they spoke of it before they left? Ryker flashed her a look, telling her to go along with him. Somehow, even after knowing him less than a day, she understood.

"Yes, and after that, we head to the village to the east, by the sea," she said.

The pair noticed how Dittmer shifted, unsettled by the new information. "Why? What is at the village by the sea?" Dittmer asked.

Astrid allowed Ryker to lead the conversation from there.

"Did we not tell you? I guess I must have forgotten in our haste to leave. There is a rumour around the settlement about a powerful witch. Apparently, she can control the sea. The Jarl wanted her, I think, to control a ship's course home. I wonder if that's where he went when he fled," Ryker said with confidence.

Dittmer halted his horse, thinking over the rumour. "Are you certain?" he asked, bracing to leave.

"Oh yes, apparently one of the Jarl's men let it slip before he perished in battle," Ryker said.

His tone was teasing, but Dittmer's love for his country and his family often blinded him. That and his hot-headed temper. Without another word, he reared his horse and galloped off towards the village in the east.

Once out of earshot, Astrid burst out in laughter. "I cannot believe he fell for that. How did you know your plan would work?" she asked, guiding her horse closer to Ryker, closing the gap created by Dittmer.

"My brother is so predictable. He lets his temper and lust for a fight blind him to the obvious," Ryker answered, leaning to the side and scooping Astrid from her horse, sitting her firmly in his lap.

"What are you doing?" Astrid giggled, feigning protest.

"Something I have wanted to do since the moment you walked out of that stream," he responded, bringing his lips down on hers. He was elated when he felt her respond, allowing his tongue to explore her mouth as she tasted him in return. Ryker wrapped his arm around her waist to secure her while keeping a tight hold of the reins. The last thing he needed was the horse to bolt and throw them off.

He allowed his free hand to explore her body, cupping her breast. It filled his hand perfectly as if it were moulded just for him. Astrid moaned at his touch, her hand exploring his chest and strong shoulders. Ryker slid his hand into her bodice, stroking her nipple. It woke at his touch, peaking, begging for more. Astrid slid her hand down, rubbing the bulge that continued to grow between his legs. She liked how it felt and wondered how it would feel inside her. Ryker sucked in a breath between his teeth at her touch. Pulling up her skirt, he skimmed his hand up her thigh and revelled at the dampness that met his fingers. He wanted it. She wanted it. Time to make it happen, he thought.

"Let's head back to your cottage and finish what we started. This is a fool's errand anyway. Sören was right. It won't result in anything noteworthy," he said flippantly, smiling against her neck as he trailed kisses down to her collar bone. Astrid arched her back and craned her neck, giving him a clear path to play.

"Oh yes, let's just run away together and ignore our responsibility," she joked back, not taking his remark seriously.

"Exactly," he growled, pulling on the reins and redirecting the horses back the way they came.

Astrid pushed back, stopping his trail of kisses. Her skin screamed to be touched, her body wanted more, but her mind knew better. She glared at him, scanning his face hoping he would begin to laugh and tell her he didn't mean it. But the longer he looked back at her with lust-filled eyes, practically salivating at the idea of her in his bed, she realised he was being serious. Or as serious as Ryker could be.

"You're being serious?" She asked in disbelief. Although she had never seen Ryker act anything other than childish, she didn't know why she expected more now.

Ryker halted the horses looking back at her in confusion. He believed she wanted the same thing he did: to roll around and enjoy the most delicious parts of one another. When Ryker failed to respond, looking at her with that dumbfounded look of ignorance and stupidity he had at the stream the day prior, her temper flared. She swatted his hand away and tugged at the arm he held around her. Once free from his embrace, she leapt off the horse, ignoring the pain shooting through her shins and ankles upon landing.

"Where are you going?" he asked, turning the horse around. She had already mounted her horse.

"You come to my home and drag me away from my chores to feed this information to Sören. You didn't think the mission was foolish or frivolous then. Did you mean any of it? Or was it all a ploy to get me alone?" she asked, staring him dead in the eye.

His expression remained unchanged. She had her answer.

"If you don't have the balls to finish this mission, I will do it without you," she said, kicking her horse into a gallop. She rode off at speed to her destination.

Ryker sat on his horse, staring after her as she thundered away, confused by what had just taken place.

CHAPTER 6

ARRIVING at the village still seething after Ryker made his silly remarks, Astrid dismounted her horse, walking it slowly past the village gates. As she walked through heading to the farm, she couldn't help the strange feeling nagging at her. Something was different, not quite right. The women, who usually waved and greeted her with a smile, shied away at her approach. They actually scurried back to their homes as though they were scared of her.

What is going on? she asked herself. Then she realised what was different, what had flustered her former friends. There was no trace of a man in sight.

Where are all the men? Surely it doesn't take a village to hunt a couple of boars? She strolled through the village square, shushing and stroking her horse's muzzle. Even the giant beast could sense the atmosphere and seem restive.

"You. Where is that idiot brother of mine?" Dittmer bellowed, storming over and leaping off his horse to face her. He pointed an angry finger at Astrid.

She groaned, rolling her eyes. "Exactly where I left him on the trail. Probably still sitting on his horse, mouth agape catching flies." Her shoulders grew tense. She really didn't want this confrontation, especially here. She was aware of Dittmer's disapproval of her, and if she were honest, she didn't particularly like him either. But he had to know this wasn't the time or place.

"You two are made for each other, never taking anything seriously. Sending me off on a wild goose chase, to what end? So you could shrug off your responsibilities? Do you have no honour?" he barked at her, getting so close she could smell his breath with every word.

"Don't talk to me about honour. I came here alone to complete a mission for you and your idiot childish brother," she snapped back, not backing down or allowing Dittmer to intimidate her. As if on cue, the cause of both their problems and frustrations trotted into the square.

"Speaking of idiots, your brother is here," she snarled, turning back to her horse, who was slowly becoming more skittish.

Ryker descended from his horse, looking between his brother and Astrid with a ridiculous grin on his face.

"It warms my heart seeing you two finally getting along," Ryker joked. Both Astrid and Dittmer shot him a look of fury as they stormed over to him.

"You are an idiot, Ryker. I have put up with your antics for years. Still, never before have you acted so irresponsibly," Dittmer barked. Turning to Astrid, he shoved an accusing finger in her face forcing her to arch away out of fear of being poked in the eye. "Not until he met you, he became much worse since you have been around. Imagine the damage he will cause, the longer he spends with you," Dittmer snarled, baring his teeth like a rabid dog.

Astrid shoved Dittmer hard. Not hard enough to make him fall, but hard enough that, by the look of shock on his face, made him take note.

"Me? No, my friend, he is an idiot all on his own. Why do you think I left him on the trail? When he is not making light of everything, his mind is only on one thing. Like a boy just discovering his manhood," she snarled between the two.

To Astrid and Dittmer's further annoyance, Ryker looked rather pleased with himself. Dittmer let out a growl. His patience had expired.

"You two are made for each other. You both make me sick. We have important tasks to carry out. The two of you have wasted enough of my time," Dittmer declared, swinging onto his horse and leaving the village.

Ryker turned back to Astrid after watching his brother pass the village gates. His eyes were once again full of lust coupled with a mischievous grin on his face. "Alone, at last, I don't think he will be back this time," he said, his voice filled with innuendo. He reached for Astrid, but she pulled away, giving him a look of death. She couldn't remember the last time her blood boiled as it did around Ryker.

"Enough!" she yelled, her voice sending a slight echo through the square. "I grow increasingly tired of your immature errant ways. It is no longer cute or fun. We have a job of utmost importance. Can you not be serious for once?" she barked, ignoring him and turning her attention back to the task at hand.

Or she would have if there had been anyone left to talk to. The square was empty. They had been in the square for several minutes, and not once had a person passed by. Her gut twisted, telling her something was very wrong. She grabbed her horse and strolled deeper into the village, following her instincts. When the farmyards came into view, she stopped. No one tended the crops. For that matter, the crops were all gone, and the land was bare. The village appeared empty, aside from the eyes of the women and children peering out through shuttered windows.

"Something's wrong," she whispered, spying Ryker at her side.

Ryker sensed it, too, finally listening to her words and acting seriously. He nodded now, his expression sombre.

"Where is everyone? Where are the men? Supplies? It appears deserted," Astrid whispered, slowly spinning, looking for the danger she could feel was near. New enforced fences had been erected around the village. The huts had fresh shutters to secure and shelter everyone inside. Ryker gripped his axe, searching and bracing himself. Then, Astrid and Ryker came to the same conclusion, and both were chilled by the realisation. Quickly, they turned to each other, "a new army," they exclaimed in unison.

The sound of gates closing, locks being latched, and the distant sound of pounding feet alerted them both. Looking in every direction, they noticed the village was being sealed up. Dread filled them both as adrenaline raced in their blood. Then, without a second thought, Ryker grabbed Astrid, lifting her with ease and throwing her on her horse's back. Ryker was no stranger to danger and, though he did not doubt Astrid's ability to defend herself, the thought of her being in harm's way vexed him. Part of him wanted to protect her and keep her safe.

"Ride, I'll catch up," he said.

Astrid had never seen Ryker look so severe, she opened her mouth to protest, but before the words rolled off her tongue, Ryker slapped her horse's backside. Her horse bolted and galloped away, easily leaping the first fence, taking Astrid right along with him.

CHAPTER 7

HER HORSE HAD ALREADY BEEN SPOOKED before Ryker smacked its rear. Now, as it galloped out of the village gates, she struggled to get it under control. *Fool, if an army is on the horizon, he will need my help,* Astrid thought.

This was not the first time a man had made an effort to shield her from danger, and it annoyed her just the same. She didn't know how many times she had to proclaim her independence to the world. She could take care of herself. Yet, deep down, she worried for Ryker. He could be facing an army alone. She was relieved when the sound of hooves behind her alerted her to his presence.

"We must get back and warn the others," Ryker yelled over the thundering of their horse's hooves. But the sound was too loud to be the pounding of their horse's hooves alone, wasn't it? They pulled the reins forcing their horses to stop. Shouting, chanting, and drums boomed around them, getting louder as it travelled towards them. They searched for which direction the sound of war came from. Much to their dismay, the sound travelled from every direction.

"Ride!" Astrid yelled, spurring her horse on, Ryker following swiftly behind.

They passed the trees not far outside the village when they were forced to stop once more. A line of soldiers blocked their path. An arrow shot past Astrid's horse's ear at great speed. It whistled as it soared through the air. Astrid twisted, trying to avoid being hit. Her horse, put off balance, reared, and she lost her grip, falling with a thud to the road. The next thing she knew, Ryker was hauling her up to her feet.

"I'm fine," she insisted, pushing him away and pulling her sword from the sheath attached to the horse's saddle.

Ryker looked her over in awe. She looked magnificent with her sword in hand, standing like a warrior queen. *My warrior queen,* he thought. Then, Astrid slapped him hard across the cheek, startling him and snapping him out of his thoughts.

"Stop gawping and fight, you fool," she yelled, charging forward, sweeping her sword upwards, slicing a soldier from gut to chin, drenching herself in his blood. Then, spinning, she swung her sword again, striking down another, before kneeling swiftly, angling her blade behind her, and impaling the soldier who loomed behind her. The man's dying cries mingled with her war cry as she yanked the sword from his gut, preparing for the next attack.

Ryker was momentarily mesmerised, dumbfounded by how outstanding and remarkable the woman before him was. His heart skipped a beat as he watched her decapitate another man. She had easily cut through at least six men before he came to his senses and charged after her. *How dare they come at my woman?!* His mind raced, fury, bloodlust, and adrenaline coursing through him, creating a fire in his veins that fuelled his rage.

A soldier approached Astrid on his horse at full speed, his sword raised high. Astrid would be defenceless if he made his strike, as she was busy fighting two soldiers. Without a second thought, he grabbed his axe and tossed it through the air. His blade sliced through the soldier's helm like a knife through butter, and his axe buried itself deep in the other man's face. The force of the impact knocked him from his horse.

Astrid's head whipped back, and she grinned seductively back at Ryker before picking up the dead soldier's sword and tossing it in Ryker's direction. He caught it with ease and used it to cut through the men blocking his path to Astrid.

Ryker's mind was in a whirl. His only thought was to protect

Astrid as his sword fell, connecting with the shoulder of the man that almost matched his size. He failed to pay attention to the soldiers charging at him from behind. As one brought his sword down, aiming to stab Ryker in the back, Astrid appeared out the corner of his eye, her sword blocking the attack. She yanked the knife from Ryker's belt with her free hand and shoved it up into the soldier's chin dragging it out and slicing his throat. The soldier gargled as he choked on his own blood, and with a swift kick to the gut, Astrid sent him flying backwards.

Ryker stood in awe. She had saved his life while he failed in his attempt to protect hers. *She truly is one of a kind*, he thought as she turned to him and smiled. Ryker couldn't help but notice how the sight of Astrid in battle roused him. He felt himself beginning to grow. Astrid stared back, panting, lust dancing in her eyes. The rising stakes, the bloodlust, it was titillating.

"Odin's beard, woman, you are going to get me killed. All I can think about is taking you here on the battlefield" he grinned, flashing her a wink. She grabbed his crotch, and he groaned in pleasure at her touch. She smirked and winked back. "Not hard enough yet. Maybe I should fight a little harder." She grinned.

She glanced over Ryker's shoulder, and Ryker glanced over hers. The charging soldiers had closed the gap. This was his chance to show off for her. He charged past her grabbing one soldier by the throat, lifting him off the ground and digging his nails in harder, watching as the man dropped his sword, grabbing at Ryker's hand, gasping for air. Ryker tossed the soldier backwards into the two men approaching, knocking them to the ground. He picked up the fallen sword. Now armed with two mighty blades, he cut through soldiers with ease.

"Ryker," Astrid yelled as she ran towards him. They were surrounded. More soldiers had joined the fight. They were vastly outnumbered, and things were beginning to look bleak.

"Grab your horse. Ride to the settlement and get my brothers," he yelled as he stabbed his sword into the gut of another fighter.

"I'm not leaving you," she protested, feeling herself becoming emotional, something that was a completely new experience for her.

"Yes, you are! Go! Now!" he yelled at her, and she couldn't help but hear the desperation in his voice. She grabbed his collar and pulled him to her kissing him deeply, her eyes filling with tears. Only reluctantly did she let him go. She broke free and ran, not looking back. She knew if she did, she would ignore his order and stay to fight.

As she galloped away from the sounds of Ryker's battle cry fading on the wind, her heart ached. *This is a mistake. He will be killed,* she thought. But what sense was there in both of them dying? She needed the other Jürgensen brothers if any of them were going to survive this.

CHAPTER 8

DITTMER LEAPT out of the way as Astrid's horse skidded to a halt, its hooves creating large trenches in the earth. Astrid jumped off her horse and ran at Dittmer, his face flushed with anger.

"Come quickly, Ryker is in trouble," she said frantically, her words almost blending together as she tried to drag Dittmer towards her horse. Dittmer pulled his arm away with ease. He simply dug in his heels and folded his arms across his chest. He looked her up and down before coughing his displeasure.

"Forget it. I'm not going anywhere with you. Whatever trouble Ryker is in this time, he can get himself out of it alone. I'm not running to save his behind again," he said, turning to leave, but not before shooting Astrid a look of disdain.

Astrid ran ahead, stopping and blocking his path. "Do you not see the blood drenching my clothes? We were ambushed. That's why there were no men in the village. There is an army heading this way. Call your men to arms and come help me save your idiot brother," she insisted, her dislike for Dittmer growing with every second. Dittmer opened his mouth to argue back, but Astrid didn't have time to waste arguing with him. She needed to get back and help Ryker. Furious and frantic, she yelled in frustration and stormed off towards Sören and Firtha's hut.

"Where do you think you are going?" Dittmer yelled after her.

"If you won't listen, Sören will," she barked back over her shoulder.

Within a few strides, Dittmer had caught up to her, grabbing her shoulder and forcing her to stop. "You will not disturb my brother with your pathetic attempt for attention," he snapped at her.

Astrid's blood boiled to the point she felt like she might burst. "I demand to speak to Sören," she growled through clenched teeth. She didn't wait for his reply. "Sören!" She screamed the name as loud as she could. If Dittmer didn't allow her to pass, she would get Sören to come to her.

"Stop! Sören is busy with more important matters right now. Firtha is in the throes of labour," Dittmer barked, shoving Astrid hard in the shoulder.

She knew she could knock him on his backside if she chose, but she decided she would save that particular pleasure for Ryker.

"Last time I checked, it was Firtha who was pushing a child out of her, not Sören," she snarled, savouring the look of horror on Dittmer's face. "Now get me, Sören!" she screamed at the top of her lungs.

She had been so intent on arguing with Dittmer that she had not noticed the attention their screams had attracted. A small crowd had begun to gather, everyone trying to figure out what was going on, some panicking. In contrast, the gathered women shouted for Astrid to hold her tongue as a child was coming into the world.

Astrid could not even breathe; she was so angry. She struggled to gather air in her lungs. Enough then. If they would not come, she would rescue Ryker for herself. Her heart raced as she launched herself back into the saddle. Her horse danced under her, ready for battle. Every emotion she had ever felt in her life flooded her at once; it was too much to take. Her heart felt as though someone had a grip on it and was squeezing the life from her. Her mind flashed with images of Ryker dead on the battlefield. Tears rained down her face uncontrollably. She wiped at them, but no sooner had she cleared them did a fresh trail of tears cut through the blood and dirt on her face. Dittmer looked at her, analysing and slowly, his face softened. His brows unfurrowed, and his mind clicked into place.

"You are telling the truth," he said softly, almost in shock.

"Of course, I am, you, clod. Ryker is in danger. We have to go now!" she cried and kicked her horse into action, not waiting to see if he followed.

CHAPTER 9

DITTMER INFORMED Sören of the news from Astrid but told him he would handle it. Sören was torn, but Firtha needed him. "I trust you. Bring our brother back, protect our home," Sören said with confidence. Dittmer gathered a troop of fighters while Astrid gathered the other sword maidens. Together, they were an unstoppable force.

The sound of their horses riding up the hills rolled like thunder. The sound of their hooves striking the ground was the Viking's drums of war. They didn't need instruments to intimidate; their skills spoke for themselves. Only they did not get far. The Viking army was stopped abruptly at the top of the hill. Their horses snorted and screamed, shying away from the fire that sped down the hill around them. It had been a dry year with little to no rain for months. The dry bush accepted the flames at an alarming rate.

"The fire is heading towards home," one of the fighters yelled. The horses panicked as their riders struggled to control them. Half of their force wanted to return home and protect their own. Firtha was having her baby. The best fighters had left with Dittmer and Astrid. The settlement residents would be sitting ducks, entirely at the fire's mercy. One by one, the men broke off riding home. They had no choice. The settlement was defenceless.

"Dittmer, go, protect our home. I will get Ryker," Astrid yelled, the sounds of the flames almost deafening as they took over more of the land. Dittmer didn't protest. With a swift nod of agreement, he turned his horse and sped off back down the hill with the rest.

"Sword maidens," Astrid yelled, calling the attention of the women in the group. "Never send a man to do a woman's job. There is an army out there, and they come for our men. They come for our children. They come for our homes," Astrid yelled, her skin pricked with goosebumps as her pulse raced with excitement. She was born to lead. "Let's show these men what Danish women are made of." She gave out a long battle cry, raising her sword high in the air. The women cheered and whooped around her, raising their swords to the sky as one.

Theirs weren't the only cheers. The voice of the army could be heard on the other side of the flames. There was no way to get to them. The only way to get to Ryker was through the fire.

"May the glory of the Valkyries be with us. It's time to strike fear into their hearts. Let's show them what happens when you mess with the sword maidens," she bellowed. Her words spoken to every woman.

The women's chorus of "Kill them!" roared over the flames, followed by chants of Astrid's name. The women cheering her name sent a chill through her, which fuelled her onwards. Astrid gathered all the air in her lungs, and her battle cry travelled on the wind. Finally, the voices on the other side of the flames quietened. They had heard her, and she knew they quaked with fear. *So they should,* she thought as she yelled for the women to charge.

The sword maidens flew through the flames, their swords raised high, and the sound of their battle cries travelled for miles. As they came out the other side, they saw the fear in the eyes of their enemies. They would regret the day they came for the Vikings. The sword maiden broke off, moving down soldiers like the wind could bend a crop. Glancing around the battlefield, sure that her fellow warriors had it under control, Astrid spurred her horse onwards. She needed to find Ryker. Gods help anyone who got in her way.

CHAPTER 10

ASTRID'S HEART filled with pride at the sight of her fellow maidens. They struck down the enemy with ease, proving that it's not just Viking men who can fight. Astrid scoured the battlefield for Ryker. The battlefield was chaos. The fire still raged, burning across the field and down the hills. A mixture of battle cries and dying gasps created a chorus of sound, exploding around Astrid. Men lay maimed and bleeding, living and dead tangled together in heaps. Chaos reigned.

A head flew across the field. Astrid whipped her head in the direction from which it came. That's when she saw him. Ryker knelt in the middle of a pile of bodies leaning on his sword. She couldn't tell if he was hurt or not, but by his stance, she knew that he was alive. She kicked her heels, spurring her horse onwards. A soldier approached Ryker from the left. Ryker had not noticed his approach, and she was too far away to stop him. She kicked her horse harder, her heart racing, pounding in time with her horse's feet. A spear stuck out of the ground like a flagpole. She leaned over the side of her horse, almost falling as she ripped it from the ground. She locked eyes on her target. *May the power of the Valkyrie guide this spear*, she prayed as she sent it flying through the air. Her prayers were answered as the spear struck the approaching enemy between the ribs, his screams alerting Ryker, who stood and finished him off with his sword. Astrid's heart fell as he staggered backwards, falling heavily to his knees.

"You are hurt," she said as she leapt from her horse, grabbing Ryker and searching for the injury. His right shoulder sat awkwardly, blood trickled from his side, and he had a nasty gash in his right thigh.

"This? No, I have had worse injuries from a beautiful sword maiden when she pushed me in the river, landing on top of me." He chuckled, wincing and holding his ribs.

"Some things never change," she protested, wrapping his arm around her shoulder and using all her strength to pull him to his feet. "Get on the horse, you fool. Ride out of here. I'll catch up," she insisted, pulling him alongside her horse. Astrid could tell he was putting on a brave face trying to hide his pain.

"I'm not leaving you," he said grimly, but Astrid was putting her foot down.

"It's your turn to run now, my love," she said, not thinking of her words before she said them. Her bones strained as she helped Ryker up onto the horse. He slumped over, offering her his hand. She swatted it away, grabbing the reins and turning the horse. She'd planned on slapping the horse's rear, the same way he had with her, but when she looked up, her heart clenched in her chest. Some of her fellow sword maidens had lost their horses. While they fought fiercely, she could see they struggled. Her friend Leonora lay lifeless on the battlefield. Things looked bleak. They were still vastly outnumbered.

"By the gods," she breathed, her voice catching in her throat as she wiped away the tears seeping from her eyes.

"If I have to die today, I go to Valhalla with honour knowing I fought my last battle with a sword maiden like no other," Ryker said, his breathing slow. She looked up at him, her heart breaking. *This can't be the ending, not before it even had a chance to start*, she thought. Ryker looked down at her with a sincere grin of admiration. But, while his lips smiled, his eyes told another story. They were sombre and filled with longing, a look she knew she echoed in her own eyes. Longing for more time.

"It's not over yet. I made a promise to your brother to get you home," she said, running ahead and stripping a fallen soldier of his bow and arrow. She clicked her tongue, and the horse slowly followed her as she sent arrows flying, clearing a path through the battlefield.

She was no longer just fighting for Ryker. She fought for her fellow maidens. She fought for justice and love. "And I'm a woman of my word," she yelled, not glancing back.

The sky filled with dark clouds, slowly turning from grey to black. The wind had begun to change. Retreat and surrender were not words in the Viking's vocabulary. They believed you fought until the end, and Astrid was determined this was not the end. A thunder-like rumble rolled up the hill, slowly the voices grew louder, and Astrid's blood raced with hope. Finally, her prayers had been answered as Dittmer, and the rest of the Viking men, burst onto the battlefield.

"Thank the gods," she whispered. She ran back to her horse, leaping on his back behind Ryker. She couldn't reach the reins around his frame.

"Ryker, grab the reins! I can't reach from here," she said, wrapping her arms around him. Sluggishly Ryker reached for the reins and sat up as straight as he could, snapping the leather and sending the horse into a trot towards Dittmer, who cleared a path through the field towards his brother.

"Retreat!" a voice yelled. The Lord's men broke ranks and began to run. Astrid cursed cowards without honour as she watched the so-called soldiers run their retreat. Too raw and untrained, they knew they were no match for the full force of the Vikings. *We will be even stronger when Ryker's brothers return,* she thought. Setting the fire was one thing, but these men had not been prepared for angry, vengeful Vikings. Plus, their plan had backfired. The wind had changed as a storm rolled in. The fire now came for Beecham's men. Cheers erupted as victory became clear.

"Are you hurt, brother?" Dittmer asked as he rode up to them. Concern laced in his voice.

"I will be fine," he groaned, slumping forward. Dittmer's face flushed with alarm. Astrid needed to get Ryker home and tend to his wounds, if she still had a home. The fire could have destroyed it.

"I will take care of him," she informed Dittmer. They locked eyes, finally coming to a common ground: their love for Ryker. Dittmer nodded. "Look after him. He acts tough, but..." he trailed off, and Astrid nodded, directing the horse onwards with a slap to its rear.

Thunder cracked, and lightning flashed, lighting a path through the black sky as heavy rains poured down around them.

Astrid was amazed the fire hadn't reached her cottage. Sorrow weighed her down as she looked over to the other homes. "So many of these homes now lay empty," she said as she slowly dismounted her horse, helping the exhausted Ryker descend. The other sword maidens had travelled back to help tend to the fire at the settlement. It didn't blaze as ferociously as it had earlier, but she could still see and smell the smoke. She hoped they could get it under control and save as much of the settlement as possible. With the help of the rain, she prayed the fire would be out soon. As she helped Ryker inside, her mind wandered to Firtha and the birth of her child. She hoped all had ended well.

Sitting Ryker down on her cot, she lit a fire in the fireplace. She filled a pot with water and set it over the flames to boil. She grabbed a needle and thread, a cloth, and more water, pulling a chair in front of Ryker. She stripped off her heavy leather armour and helped Ryker out of his drenched clothes. She was relieved to see his wounds were minor. Apart from the gash on his thigh, he had a few cuts and bruises and maybe a broken rib or two. Nothing he couldn't heal from with some time and rest. Ryker was exhausted. He had fought so many for so long.

"How did you manage to fight for so long and come out without more serious wounds?" she asked, cleaning up his cuts.

"It was you. I couldn't allow myself to be killed without seeing your face one last time," he answered, wincing as she pulled the thread through his skin, stitching together his wound.

Looking up through her lashes, she finally confessed what was in her heart.

"I was terrified I had lost you. My heart ached when I spied you on the field." She choked, reliving the terror she felt.

"You are not rid of me yet," he said, his voice rough and low. "You saved my life more times than I can count today. Everybody I lay to waste was so I could get back to you. As the numbers increased, I was terrified you hadn't made it out of the battlefield in time. The thought of what those men would do if they got their hands on you...."

A stray tear fell from his eye and landed on her hand as she tied the last stitch. She rested a hand on his looking up, repeating his words back to him. "You are not rid of me yet," she said with a wink.

"You were magnificent, so strong, and skilled with every weapon you lay your hands on. I would be honoured to call you to mine...." he said, watching her face. He half expected her to protest or slap him across the face, but instead, she gazed back with love in her eyes. "I love you, Astrid. There is no other way to explain it. And it feels so good to say the words out loud finally. I love you." He smiled.

Blinking back tears, she stood, looking down at him with love. She cupped his face in her hands, pulling his ear to her chest so he could hear that her heartbeat was only for him.

"I love you too, you childish fool," she said, wrapping her arms around him.

"I am *your* childish fool," he said back, wrapping his arms around her and holding her tight.

"That you are," she chuckled, but Ryker could also hear the possession in her voice. They had claimed each other. He was hers, and she was his.

Ryker stood and kissed Astrid with a passion he didn't know he had. It was a passion he never wanted to fade and a passion he would die for. To his surprise, even injured, Ryker wanted more. No. He *needed* more. Lust, love, and the adrenaline from battle made an intoxicating combination in his blood. When she'd voiced her feelings, it spurred him on even further. He needed her. To show her how much she meant to him. Standing to his full height, he helped her out of her wet clothes, finally gazing upon the body he had only seen through her shift that day in the stream. The body he had fantasised about since that moment.

Her beasts sat proudly on her chest. While she is slender and muscular, she had wide hips that Ryker couldn't wait to grip. He loved her ample round backside and wanted to sink his teeth into the glorious flesh.

Astrid likewise marvelled at Ryker as she removed the last of his clothes, revealing the god-like body underneath. Slowly, he brought her down onto the cot with him. As he gazed down at her, his every nerve came alive.

She is mine, and I am hers, he thought.

Their bodies intertwined, and they explored each other, tasting each other, savouring every inch. Astrid growled seductively, the sound rumbling at the back of her throat as Ryker kissed, sucked, and licked every inch of her, igniting her body. His groin ached as the size grew at the sight of her. Slowly he entered her, enjoying every second, every inch. Their lovemaking was slow and passionate, yet filled with fire, and when they gained their release together, neither could think of anything in the world that felt so good.

EPILOGUE

Sören, Ryker, and Astrid rode up a neighbouring hill. They sat astride their horses, watching as Beecham's Castle burned. His home for theirs. Justice. The settlement had taken heavy damage. It was going to take a while to repair it to its former glory. It wouldn't be ready in time for their brothers' return from Denmark. To Sören's surprise and gratefulness, Ryker appeared to have set aside his childish ways. His mind now focused on the task at hand.

"We were not supposed to start an all-out war," he reminded the others.

"We did not start this; they attacked first," Astrid said, fury in her voice and revenge in her heart. For Ryker, for our home, and for Leonora, she thought, keeping her new mission in life in the forefront of her mind.

Sören was furious. Ryker and Dittmer had never seen him in such a state, and they had witnessed some of his worst fits of anger over the years. "They brought this on themselves," Sören said. Beecham's men had put his wife and child in immediate danger. That was a crime that needed paying for. Sören had determined the price would be steep.

"Dittmer, bring the prisoners. We will get out our answers once and for all," Sören said as he watched Dittmer and his men hauling Lord Beecham and his family, bound in chains, walking behind their horses. Sören followed Dittmer and their men home, keeping a close eye on their enemy from behind, leaving Astrid and Ryker alone at the top of the hill.

"What do we do now?" Astrid asked.

Ryker hauled her off her horse once again. He let his hands slide over every inch of her as he set her on his lap. She chuckled, giving him a flash of her childish side.

"We love one another. Beyond that? We go where we need." He grinned, bringing his lips down to hers. His hands slipped under her skirts as her hand stroked the bulge at his groin. They explored each other as best they could while sitting on horseback. When their passion burned like the fire in Beecham's Castle, they dismounted. They stumbled as they tore at each other's clothing, intent on possessing each other completely. The force of their desire would make the gods envious.

Pinned against a tree, Astrid wrapped her legs around Ryker's waist and marvelled at his girth and length as he finally thrust into her. Nestled inside, he paused and rested his forehead on hers, connecting with her. Then, over the screams of Beecham's men trapped in the castle, Ryker and Astrid shouted each other's names as they reached the height of their pleasure together.

THE END

DITTMER
ENCHANTED BY THE GODDESS

PROLOGUE

THE SETTLEMENT RESIDENTS wiped the sweat from their brows and stretched out their aching backs. Weeks had passed since the fire almost destroyed everything they held dear. Fall approached, and they needed to make sure they had supplies enough for winter before the cold set in. Thankfully, while the damage had been substantial, the Danes were resilient people, and they still had enough numbers to rebuild.

In the centre of the settlement sat the hut the Jürgensen brothers once used for counsel and battle plans. It now housed their prisoners, what remained of Beecham and his family. The hut stood guarded day and night.

Sören, Dittmer, and Ryker walked past their *visitors'* new home, checking on the guards to ensure everything was still as it should be. Once satisfied that Beecham and his family were safe, secure, well-fed, and watered, they walked on, checking on the progress of the rebuild. There was also much to discuss regarding the information they had managed to obtain thus far. What there was of it.

"We have been questioning Beecham for weeks. How do we only know what we already knew? Skimming money off the top of the Danegeld is hardly a reason to kill a man or start a war with his family. There has to be something we're missing. What else is he hiding?"

Dittmer groaned. He was becoming increasingly impatient with every day that passed with no new developments.

"I think a better question is how do we get that information? The threat of torture doesn't seem to scare that man," Ryker said, kicking a small rock and sending it flying several feet ahead.

"Actions speak louder than words," Dittmer said with a slightly wicked grin.

"No brother, he is the monster, *we* are not," Sören insisted.

"I was making light, brother, since Ryker appears to have lost his sense of humour," Dittmer replied with a careless wave of his hand.

"Not the time, brother," Ryker whispered back.

They walked talking strategy, trying to determine Beecham's weakness so they could exploit it and get the information they needed. The discussion of threatening his wife and children was passed around again. In the end, they all agreed it was a bad idea. Beecham knew that Sima had run away with her Viking, Abjörn, out of love. This also meant he knew they could hardly act on any threat to Beecham's family. Abjörn, the eldest, would have his brothers' heads if they so much as laid a finger on Sima's mother or siblings.

"It's like Beecham is scared to speak. I suspect he awaits his King. Perhaps that is who he truly fears," Ryker said, his expression uneasy.

If that were true, their battle was bigger than they thought. The brothers lapsed into silence. War with all of Britain was not something any of them cared to indulge in. Whatever happened next, they needed to resolve this before the King became involved.

Their conversation was interrupted when a rider approached. His horse was blowing hard at the speed at which he galloped. As the rider drew closer, Dittmer recognised the rider as being one of the men who had been sent out on patrol only that morning.

"Do you have news?" Sören asked, his brow furrowed deep.

"We have found the Jarl Halfden," the rider spoke as he patted his horse's neck, allowing his steed a moment to rest.

"Where?" Ryker asked a little more forcefully than he intended.

"We patrolled the coast and found him there. He prepares a small fleet of ships on the other side of the hills. He must have thought he would be out of sight of the settlement, and we wouldn't find him. But we have." The rider spoke with satisfaction while his horse snorted and pawed at the ground.

"How many?" Dittmer asked, feeling his blood race.

"Three ships," the rider spoke with a grim smile, sensing what Dittmer planned next.

Finally, some action! Dittmer ran to grab his horse, shouting to his men who followed his command. "Come men! The Jarl awaits!" His voice boomed out over the settlement.

His men scrambled, cheering their response as they grabbed their weapons and readied their horses. Dittmer could see his brothers, Sören and Ryker, were not far behind.

They would stop him upon the beach if need be.

CHAPTER 1

THESSALY HAD BEEN GIVEN to the Jarl Halfden as a gift. He then gave her to his Vikings. That was after she was presented to Lord Beecham. She had exchanged hands so many times she had lost count. She hated her life as a slave but ensured she was useful. Otherwise, they might use her for unthinkable things. A slave's life was no life. *But there are always others worse off than yourself.* She told herself this every night before she went to sleep.

The primary role in her new life was as a cook's assistant. It wasn't much of a job, being one anyone could do. She worried that she didn't hold much value and could easily be traded to someone much worse than the Vikings if she wasn't so useful with her hands. Fabric bent to her will. Her skill was unmatched. It might not seem like much of a skill to others, but her ability to mend sails to the point they appeared almost new is what kept her in a somewhat comfortable life.

Knowing her worth aboard their ships, she was safe from unwanted advances. The men aboard were under threat of death if she were harmed. That didn't stop the lingering looks and crude comments. She had had her fill with the men telling her all the ways they wanted her, and rolled her eyes when they exposed themselves, trying to tempt her. Even if they did pose a size to tickle her fancy, she would rather jump overboard and be lost to the sea than lay with any of them. She was their prisoner, after all, but not their whore.

Thessaly had spent the best part of the day mending yet another sail. It baffled her how they managed to tear so many. She suspected it had to do with what a crude lot of men the Jarl employed. They were careless with their tools and supplies, and inattentive when doing their work. She wondered if such traits might be to her advantage someday and resolved to keep a careful watch. With this thought in mind, she nodded and folded the sail after inspecting her work before taking it up to the deck to be hoisted back up where it belonged. Halfden's men had been preparing the ships for a long voyage for the last few weeks, and they were almost ready to set sail. To where she had no idea.

She stepped out onto the deck, searching for the right man to hand the sail to when a noise from the shore caught her attention. A small army of Vikings on horseback and foot charged towards the ship. Arrows flew through the air tearing the sails which were already aloft.

"I just repaired that sail," Thessaly complained as she watched the mainsail shred to pieces.

Halfden's men engaged in battle as men fought to come aboard the ship. Chaos erupted around her as men appeared from every corner of the vessel, brandishing weapons, and barging past her. Her heart pounded, and her mouth went dry. Terrified, she spied boxes and barrels of supplies not yet taken below deck. She ducked down behind them, ensuring she still had a clear view of what was going on.

She crouched both fascinated and terrified. Men on both sides were brutes. They sliced through each other as though they were glad to do so. Blood coated the deck near her as several arrows embedded themselves in the chest of one of the men on deck. The deck trembled under Thessaly's feet as his large form landed heavily in a pile. As he bled out, his blood flowed freely, a river of gore coming ever nearer. She scrunched up into a tighter ball, trying to avoid it.

As she tried to escape the blood of the dead that seemed to chase her across the deck, a thought occurred to her. *Escape.* These strange English shores may not be the beautiful land of Greece that she once called home, but it was better than life aboard that ship where she was only a slave. She peeked over the side of the boat, looking for the best direction she could run.

Over the hills? Too open. Along the coast? That's where these other

Vikings came from. Into the woods? Who knows what creatures called it their home? Her mind raced. That was when her eyes landed on him. A giant of a man impossible to ignore, young but strong. He fought valiantly. She noticed how he made waves through the battlefield, causing enough distraction that the men aboard began to run to join the battle on land.

Her heart raced and joy filled her being as the shores of England spoke to her. Called her. *Freedom.*

She prepared to run. She planned to head through the woods, then over the hills where the Jarl's ships could not follow. She stood, slowly making her way across the boat, trying not to look suspicious when a yell pulled at her. She could hear many cries of pain, but this one spoke to her, drawing her attention despite herself. She looked back over her shoulder and watched as the valiant Viking she admired moments before fell to the ground.

CHAPTER 2

IN ALL THE CHAOS, Thessaly hadn't noticed the Jarl appear on deck. She jumped as he barked orders behind her. The attackers were outnumbered, and as they ran for reinforcements, Halfden hurried his men back to the ships.

"Back to the ships! Prepare to set sail before they return," he barked, his voice booming could no doubt be heard even at the far end of the beach. As his men obeyed their orders, the Jarl's following command turned Thessaly's blood to ice.

"Round up the slaves. Anyone who does not serve a purpose to our course, kill," he yelled, storming down the steps towards her hiding place.

She knew she was safe, her skill with mending sails would be much needed on their journey, but that didn't stop her from trembling with fear. Tears flooded her eyes as she watched the terrified slaves on shore try to fight back and run only to have their throats slit or their heads bashed in. These people may not be from her homeland. She may not have known them very well or at all. But she mourned each one as if they were her blood. These people were innocent, and their deaths were meaningless and cruel.

This man is pure evil, Thessaly thought as her heart ached in her chest. She forced herself not to turn away. She would watch if these people were to be murdered in cold blood and lost to history. As life slipped from their eyes, she made a mental note of their faces. *You did not die alone,* she prayed, hoping the dead could hear her and gain peace.

Halfden was not finished yet.

"Kill the wounded too. They slow us down, and I will not have them captured and reveal anything to our enemy," he shouted, his face screwed up in anger and disgust as he stepped in the blood spilt by his hand. Shaking the blood off his boot, he yelled to his men to stop. Thessaly followed the Jarl's line of sight and watched as he examined the unconscious body of the giant man. It took three of the Jarl's men to hold him up.

"The sigil. Look what we have here, boys. The youngest Jürgensen," he yelled for all his men to hear. His face finally broke into a smile. Thessaly much preferred his face clouded over with anger; his smile terrified her.

"Take him to the hold. I have use for him," Halfden sneered, leading his men back on board.

Thessaly looked back over to the shore; she could still escape. The coast was clear. But she turned to face the prisoner, something called to her. She only had moments to make her decision. The plan formed in her mind quickly. Before the Jarl came aboard, she kept low and hurried down to the hold, hiding in the shadows behind crates of supplies. She held her breath as the three men tossed the prisoner down the stairs. He landed with a painful thud only a few feet from where she cowered. She moved in the shadows to get a better view as they dragged him to his feet and tied him to a support beam.

Once she was sure the men were back on deck, she crept out of the shadows. After all the horrors she had witnessed that day, all the death and pain, she needed to know if he was alive or another victim of Halfden's evil. Keeping an eye on the door in case someone came back, she cupped the prisoner's face with her hands as she examined him. His face was wet with sweat. Blood trickled from the corner of his mouth. She watched him carefully as the lanterns hanging around the hold cast a soft light upon his face.

He had chiselled features, a strong jaw, and a broad nose. She traced a small scar over his right eye, and he let out a small groan. Thessaly let out a sigh of relief.

"Thank the gods," she whispered. Her heart could not take another death this day.

CHAPTER 3

DITTMER BEGAN TO WAKE. His head pounded, and his vision blurred. All he could see was darkness and the poorly lit silhouette of a woman. He felt her hand on his face and liked how it felt. He found himself leaning into the caress as he drifted in and out of consciousness.

"Finally, I have reached the halls of Valhalla. Tell me the name of the one who greets me," he said, his voice barely a whisper.

Thessaly tried to wake him. She stepped a little closer to whisper in his ear, so as to not alert the men up on deck.

"My name is Thessaly. I need you. I need you to wake up," she whispered, heart racing in the beginnings of true panic.

His masculine scent filled her nose, and she closed her eyes, inhaling it, finding calm and peace in the scent.

Dittmer turned his head slightly, in the direction of the sweet voice speaking to him. The accent was different. Not a Danish accent as he thought would greet him, but he was happy all the same.

"I am Dittmer, the youngest of the Jürgensen brothers. Does, a brave warrior like myself, get a welcoming kiss as I enter Valhalla after my troubled journey?" He rambled, puckering his lips and turning his face toward hers.

Thessaly almost obliged before she pulled back. She slapped him across the face trying to wake him and make him see where he truly was – the hold of Halfden's ship, not the halls of Valhalla.

When he groaned, his face crumpling at the sting of her hand across his cheek, she sighed. Frustrated and needing his help, she looked around. The light from the hatch above, which had not been correctly sealed, shone on the ropes binding him.

She studied the ropes, untangling the knots in her mind. She had a puzzle back home in Greece when she was a little girl that made freeing Dittmer child's play. The hardest part was pulling the ropes free. Dittmer was considerably taller than Thessaly, and she had to stand on her tiptoes to reach his wrists above his head. His weight pulled the binds tighter, but thankfully she managed to get him free.

Suddenly, with nothing holding him upright, he fell forward, right into Thessaly's arms. She stumbled and fell to the floor, trapped beneath his great hulking weight. Startled by the fall, Dittmer slowly came around, leaning up on one arm, and rubbing the bump on his head with the other.

Thessaly looked up at his face. Now he was awake, and she could look deep into his stunning green eyes. As he tried to get his bearings, he moved around on top of her, seeming oblivious to her presence beneath him. As he rubbed against her, she couldn't help but feel aroused. She liked how he felt on top of her.

"Hey, do you mind getting up? I can't move." She smirked, pushing herself free.

"Where am I?" he asked, finally looking at her, his face awash with confusion.

"Halfden's ship. You are in the hold," she replied, standing upright and straightening her dress. Dittmer's eyes lingered over her. Her dress was ripped from ankle to thigh, exposing her beautiful olive skin. Her hair was long down her back and as bright as the sun.

Snapping back into reality, her words sank in, his face hardened, as he drew himself up and marched towards the stairs behind her.

"Where are you going?" she asked, her voice hushed.

"To kill Halfden," he snarled. His vision tunnelled on the door as his new mission cemented in his mind.

Thessaly wrapped both her hands around his bulging bicep and used all her weight to try and pull him back. It was no use. He was too strong. She ran in front of him, blocking his path. Finally, he stopped and stared down at her. Her eyes pleaded with him not to get himself killed.

Something about her deep brown eyes connected with him, and he stood ready to listen.

"Don't be a fool. You are alone and unarmed. There are far too many of them up there. Stop and think, would you?" she insisted, tapping his temple.

Dittmer held back a smirk. Something about her made him want to laugh, and now was no time for laughing.

Footsteps from above alerted them both. Thessaly began to breathe heavily, her eyes widened in panic.

"Someone is coming. Quickly, get back where you were. We need to make it look like you are still bound. If they find out I helped you, I will be killed just like the other slaves, and I'm not ready to die just yet."

She hurried, pushing him back with everything she had, but it was no use. Dittmer was unmoving. She looked up into his eyes, tears brimming her lashes.

"Please," she begged, reaching a hand up to touch his face, the way she had when he'd first awoken.

Her touch seemed to call him back. He stared at her and found her eyes hypnotic. Whatever she wanted, he would do. Dittmer agreed, with no further hesitation, as they both scrambled to make it look like he had not been freed. He watched Thessaly sneak off into the shadows and lost her location as she faded into the shadows. It impressed him how she could hide so skilfully.

CHAPTER 4

DITTMER READIED himself for the attack when a young boy came down the stairs. He was dressed as all the others were, so Dittmer knew he was one of the Jarl's men rather than a slave. The boy must have been in his teen years and looked scared as he approached Dittmer carrying a tray of food.

"I was ordered to bring you this. It is not much, but we must keep you fed and watered. The Jarl does not want you to die of starvation," the young boy stammered.

"And how do you propose I eat with my hands bound above my head?" Dittmer asked. A slight grin twitched. Of course, he was not truly bound. Not anymore, thanks to the beautiful Thessaly.

The boy stood frozen in thought. "I…. uhm…. I can't unbind you. You might attack me," he stammered, and the tray he carried shook in his trembling hands.

Dittmer wondered how the lad had become involved with the Jarl. He was clearly scared of his own shadow; he wouldn't last five minutes in a real fight. Tall but all skin and bone, Dittmer doubted if he could even lift a sword.

"I could feed you," the boy said, very pleased with his idea as he set the tray down on top of a nearby barrel.

"Ha!... I'd rather starve," Dittmer chuckled, glaring at the boy, his eyes locked on his.

"You may change your mind later when your stomach growls. Just don't wait too long, it will go cold, and the rats might eat it for you," the boy said before leaving.

"Wait, how old are you?" Dittmer asked as curiosity got the better of him.

"Fourteen," the boy replied.

"How did you get involved with the Jarl? You don't look like you have the strength to lift a knife, let alone a sword," Dittmer said.

The boy's face suddenly became sad, and his eyes dropped to the floor. Curious, Dittmer decided he needed to hear more from the boy. Partly because he needed information on the type of men Halfden kept in his command, partly because he felt sorry for the boy.

"You know, I am a little hungry. Can you give me some of that bread?" Dittmer asked, angling his head towards the food. He had to admit the smell was making him hungry.

The boy carefully broke off a piece holding it close for Dittmer to take it from him. Once the boy realised that Dittmer would not bite off his hand, he spoke. "I'm good with a bow. I can shoot a squirrel in the eye from a fair distance," he said with pride, giving Dittmer a second bite of bread. "Truly, I'm a hostage…well…a slave, but I refuse to use that word," he said before a voice from the deck startled him.

"Sorry, I must go. I'm needed on deck," he said frantically, running up the stairs, tripping over his feet before closing the door behind him and locking it tightly.

A slave who wears the Jarl's armour? If he is good with a bow or not, slaves are generally used as servants. Halfden must not have the forces we assumed, Dittmer thought, his mind racing with confusion.

Thessaly crept out from the shadows. Dittmer was so lost in thought that he had forgotten she was there until he saw her.

"I sense your confusion. What would you like to know?" she asked as Dittmer lowered his arms, stretching his bulging shoulders to unkink the knots.

"Dose the Jarl have many slaves?" Dittmer asked, finally caving and tucking into his food. He was surprised by how good it tasted. He offered Thessaly some bread, and she accepted it happily.

She sighed deeply before she began her story. "Not as many as he used to. Not after today anyway," she said, and Dittmer heard the sorrow in her words.

"What do you mean?" he asked, popping some cheese into his mouth.

"After you and your forces attacked, Halfden ordered the wounded and any slaves without purpose to be killed. He didn't want them to slow him down or risk being captured and spill information to his enemies," Thessaly said. She saw all the slaves being mercilessly killed as she closed her eyes. The memory stabbed at her.

"Why were you spared?" Dittmer asked.

"I come from a land called Greece. I was taken as a slave for my weaving abilities. Did you see those sails? I mended them all when others thought they were unusable."

Dittmer tossed her words around in his mind. He had heard of her homeland and knew it was far to the south but had never had the chance to travel so far from home.

"I didn't think the Jarl had been so far at sea. When did he travel to Greece?" Dittmer asked, wondering just how many other such treasures the man had acquired.

"He didn't. I was taken by slave traders and travelled to England. I was given to the King, who then gave me as a gift to Lord Beecham as thanks for making the coastline secure. After that, Lord Beecham gave me as a gift to The Jarl for his help," she finished.

Her words startled Dittmer. Securing the coastline? What about the settlement? How had Beecham secured the coast?

"How can that be? The settlement my people call home is on the coast. That line of the coast belongs to the Vikings," Dittmer said, his brow furrowed so deep it almost touched his nose. He couldn't wrap his head around anything she was saying. He blamed the bump on his head for his confusion as he stroked the still tender spot on the back of his head.

"No, Lord Beecham got rid of the Viking leader. Beecham gave goods, gold, me, and a few other slaves to Halfden in exchange for gaining an exit of all Vikings from the coast." Thessaly was frowning as she spoke.

Her explanation only left Dittmer more confused. The settlement still stood. What she said explained why the Jarl was leaving; he had been bribed. But where did that leave the settlement? What did that mean for Dittmer and his brothers? He looked over to Thessaly, her arms wrapped around her as she shivered. The sun was starting to set, and what little light they had was leaving the cabin.

"You're shivering. Come here, we can share body heat under my furs," Dittmer said, sitting against a box and pulling his furs from around his shoulders. Thessaly looked at him, confusion and concern in her eyes.

"I don't bite," he chuckled. Slowly she walked over, like a scared lamb approaching a wolf. Tentatively, she sat by him but was still at arm's length. Rolling his eyes, Dittmer pulled her to him and draped his furs over the two of them. The motion of the boat rocking seemed to calm her as she slowly snuggled herself deeper under his arm, resting her head on his chest.

CHAPTER 5

THE DAY GAVE way for the night, and the cold air from the sea crept in through the gaps around the hatch of the wooden ship. Thessaly huddled closer to Dittmer. The few lanterns that hung around the hold had begun to burn out, giving them little to no light. Thessaly shivered; not from the cold, but from the thoughts running through her mind about the beast of a man she clung to and the feel of his rough hands around her.

"You are still shivering," he commented before pulling her onto his lap and cocooning them in his furs. As he pulled her tight into him, his hand grazed her thigh through the slit in her dress. He liked the feel of her skin. It was like running his fingers over silk.

Dittmer also noted how her breathing had become heavy. He knew what that meant. She was either attracted to him or afraid of him. By the way her hands explored his chest and arms, he had his answer.

"What are you doing?" he asked, looking into her eyes as she ran her hands up and down his shoulders and across his chest. She gazed up at him without fear, her eyes glazed over with a hint of lust.

"I'm trying to keep you warm like you are with me," she replied, her voice so low that he could have missed her words had he not been listening for them. Her breathy syllables mingled with the slosh of the waves and the creaks of the ship as it moved on the water. He nodded and ran his hand up and down her legs, up her back, and froze at her chest.

She trembled at his touch, tilting her head back and closing her eyes, allowing her senses to let her feel every movement. Thessaly rested her head on his shoulder, craning her neck that she might press her lips softly to his collar bone and then his neck.

Liking the feeling of her lips on his skin he inhaled deeply, savouring her scent. He lifted her hand to his lips, trailing soft tender kisses up her arm, her shoulder, her neck.

Thessaly hummed deep in the back of her throat. Dittmer paused. He was enjoying being so close to her and experiencing her in a way he had never experienced someone before. He was not unaware this was a bad idea for both of them. Dittmer was proud to be a Viking and had always planned on taking a Viking wife when the time was right. At the same time, this woman held a beauty he had never seen and bravery he admired. If she were caught helping him, she would surely be put to death.

Reluctantly, he admitted to himself that he couldn't allow things to go any further between them.

If he was to lay with her, he didn't want to force her, like he imagined others had. The life of a slave was well known. The horrors of what men did to them were spoken about in hushed tones in every land. If he ever chose to lay with her, he wanted her to want it too.

Thessaly cupped his face in her hands and gently rubbed her nose across his. As she leaned in for a kiss, he pulled away.

"What's wrong?" she asked, a little startled by his change of heart. He had seemed to be enjoying himself only moments before.

"I will not force you. I will not simply take what I want. I am a man of honour," he said, more so for himself than to answer her question. In his mind, he made these words a mantra, a reminder to himself why this was a bad idea.

Thessaly examined his features as his face turned to stone. She pulled back, climbing out of his lap hurriedly, wrapping the edge of his fur around her. She turned her back to him, a little insulted.

"You were not forcing me. I was willing," she whispered.

It was clear she had not intended Dittmer to hear, but he did. Dittmer rolled on his side, facing away from her, unsure of what to do. Uneasily, they both tried to get some sleep. Tomorrow was another day and would hold new challenges.

Tired as they were, rest did not come easily for either of them.

CHAPTER 6

THESSALY COULD HEAR Dittmer's soft snores as he drifted off into a deep sleep. But sleep eluded her. Tired, unsettled, and full of pent-up energy, she couldn't shake her earlier encounter with him under his furs. So, she decided to make herself useful. She searched for supplies they could use while they held up in the hold: a blanket, dried fish, anything to make their time together a little more tolerable.

As she worked, she wandered closer to the hatch. Voices above deck caused her to freeze. She recognised one of the voices. It was Halfden. Slowly, she crept up the stairs, listening closely at the door.

"I believe you two are going around doubting your leader? Asking one too many questions?" Halfden's voice said. Thessaly didn't need to see his face. She could hear the evil smirk through the wood.

"No, Sir," one voice stammered, the man's fear transferring to Thessaly as she began to understand how close she was to what was fast becoming a very dangerous situation. She began to tremble, and her pulse raced.

"Oh, so now you lie to me." Halfden chuckled. Thessaly knew that chuckle. It was Halfden's tell. He made that sound every time he planned on doing something that turned her stomach. Bile rose in her throat.

"They have been questioning how you intend to become the new King of Denmark," Njal – Halfden's second in command – said. Thessaly recognised his voice instantly. No one spoke. In some ways, the silence was more terrifying than the evil intention in Halfden's words. Finally, the silence was broken.

"Our prisoner down there is the youngest son to the family who is heir to the current King," Halfden began. Thessaly could hear his footsteps as he slowly paced back and forth. "The King's sons, the next rightful heirs to the throne...mysteriously died, all under different and tragic.... unanswerable conditions," Halfden continued.

"The Jürgensen brothers will be so distracted by their missing brother and rebuilding that monstrosity they call home that they are paying no attention to what they should. While they scurry around like insects, I will travel back to Denmark and kill the King." Halfden informed them.

Thessaly put her hand over her mouth as she gasped in shock at what she was hearing.

"That is all well and good Sir, but what about the next heir? What is his name?.... Abjörn?" Njal asked in a mocking tone.

"I'm so glad you asked Njal. In their scramble to find him...they simply won't," Halfden said, and Thessaly could hear the smile in his voice; her blood ran cold. But she couldn't pull herself away. She needed to listen to the rest of his plan so she had something to tell Dittmer. This information could be important to him.

"Three ships...two missions. I will go to Denmark and take care of this King, while the other two vessels will circle around to the other side of the settlement. Yes, it will take a little longer than sailing there directly...but they would see us coming from the direct route. From the other side of the settlement, they will be blindsided by the attack," he said, his pacing stopped abruptly, but his words carried on.

Njal chuckled. "My Jarl, these cowering fools know your plan.... every.... last....detail."

"That's right," Halfden said in mock surprise. He fell silent for a moment. "Kill them," he ordered.

Thessaly didn't wait around to hear their screams for mercy or for the bodies to fall. Forgetting about supplies, she ran down the steps to a sleeping Dittmer. Frantically, she shook him, trying to wake him. He needed to hear the Jarl's plan before it was too late.

CHAPTER 7

"WAKE UP, DITTMER, WAKE UP," Thessaly insisted, swatting him repeatedly when he refused to wake.

"It's Dittmer, now let me sleep," he groaned, pulling his furs tighter around him.

"Dittmer, it's Halfden! You have to wake up," she said, standing and kicking him up the backside.

Dittmer jumped to his feet, Thessaly took a step back, unsure if the anger on his face was targeted at her forceful attempts to wake him or at the news of Halfden.

"What about Halfden?" he snorted himself awake.

Thessaly told him everything she had overheard and everything she knew about his second-in-command, Njal. She informed him that Njal was just as evil and vindictive as Halfden. It was probably why they got along so well. Dittmer looked around, opening boxes and barrels, searching for anything he could use as a weapon.

"What are you doing? They will hear you," she said, grabbing him, trying to make him stop. He was making so much noise that she was sure a heavily armed guard would rush through the door and catch them both at any moment.

"I must stop him," he said, shrugging out of her grasp.

"You are going to get us both killed. Please stop and think for a minute," she pleaded, tugging at his arm again. This time he stopped and turned to her; his face red with rage. Seeing her scared face, he softened. He hadn't meant to worry her, but he needed to stop Halfden.

"You can't go up and fight, there are far too many. Besides, you don't have a weapon." Her voice was a whisper. "What do you think he has done with your brother? What did he call him?" she asked, scouring her memory for the name.

"Abjörn? I'm not worried about him. Firstly, he is the best warrior I know. He taught me how to fight and use every weapon possible. He is already in Denmark. Let the Jarl head there. Abjörn will kill him," he said with a smirk as if he was already watching his brother strike down the Jarl in his mind.

"You hardly seem worried. What about the other ships?"

"If I know my brothers, they will already have reinforcements chasing us down. Our ships are many compared to Halfden's pathetic fleet. I just need to slow them down enough so they can catch up before the other ships turn towards the settlement," he said, heading past her to the door.

She grabbed for his arm again, sliding along behind him as his force was no match for her.

"Please, it's not just his men up there. There are other slaves like me. Think of them. They will likely be killed in the crossfire if you attack," she begged.

Dittmer stopped, conflicted. He knew what he needed to do. He knew what he wanted to do, but her words stabbed him like a dagger through the heart. Halfden had killed slaves just to prevent being slowed down. Innocent people would likely be killed again if Halfden simply lost his temper or thought one of them helped him. That's when his mind flashed to Thessaly, wrapped in his arms. She would likely be killed too. While Dittmer lived for the fight and wanted his revenge, he never killed anyone without purpose, and he was not about to let innocent blood be spilt because he acted too soon.

"I have an idea," Thessaly said suddenly, grabbing his arm with excitement.

Dittmer turned to face her with curious amusement. What plan could she have that might help them?

"What is made can be unmade," she said with a smile.

Dittmer still didn't follow her train of thought. He cocked a brow questioningly, folded his arms, and waited for her to fill him in on the grand idea that brought her so much glee.

"I mended those sails. I can tear them apart just as easily." She smiled, and Dittmer realised he liked seeing her smile. She had a dimple on each cheek when her smile took over her face. He also liked how quickly she blended her own escape mission with his revenge. She had been traded from pillar to post, probably experienced unimaginable things, but life had not broken her. *Strong like a Viking woman*, he thought.

"It's too dangerous. What if you are caught?" he asked, suddenly realising he didn't want her in harm's way.

"I am a slave on this ship. I often go up the mast to check all is good with the sails. No one will suspect a thing," she insisted.

Giving it another moment's thought, Dittmer smiled back at her. It was a good plan. If she could bring down the sails, his brothers would catch up in no time. He could also use the distraction to sneak about the ship and take out as many men as he could.

"Thessaly, you are brilliant. This plan could work. I will sneak up to the deck and stay hidden. I will protect you if anyone suspects," he said, her excitement becoming infectious.

"What can I say? I watched you fight before they took you down. Your bravery and quick thinking in battle inspired me," she beamed.

Dittmer cocked a brow and his chest puffed up with pride. She had been watching him? This was new. He liked the idea of her spying on him, admiring his valour. What else about him had he inspired in her? His mind wandered over the possibilities.

He took a step closer to her, cupping her face with his hand and placing the other against the small of her back, bringing her closer to him. He towered over her, and she had to arch her back and crane her neck to look him in the eyes.

"Are you still willing?" he breathed.

She looked up at him, reaching up to his collar bone – as high as she could – "yes," she whispered with a smile.

Dittmer leaned down, so she didn't have to strain her neck much more. He gently pressed his lips to hers and welcomed the kiss she gave in return when she could finally wrap her arms around his neck. Her tongue invaded his mouth, and he massaged her tongue in return, running his hand around the back of her neck stroking her hair. He noticed how she held back a chuckle. Her neck must be ticklish. He broke apart and cradled her neck, lost in her eyes.

Dittmer had always been so set in his plan to marry a Danish girl who shared his love for danger and shared the same values. Yet as he got lost in Thessaly's gaze, he couldn't imagine finding a girl he wanted more than her. The thought startled him. His stomach flipped, and for the first time, he understood when women said they felt as though their insides were filled with butterflies when they were with the right man. It was a feeling of excitement like no other, as he realised that he liked the idea of her being his.

"We will continue this later," he smiled, finally letting her go and stepping back.

"Even though I am not a Dane?" she asked with a mischievous grin. Dittmer stood frozen, transfixed by her words. How did she know his thoughts? Was she a witch? Could she read his mind? He watched her grab a small handbasket and fill it with food supplies from a barrel. She would look less suspicious if she seemed to be in the middle of chores.

"How did you?...." he started, stopping himself, amazed and a little worried by her. She chuckled, looking over her shoulder as she approached the door.

"You mumble in your sleep," she winked, turning and waving her hands mockingly. "She beautiful, but I need Danish bride," she said in as masculine a voice as she could muster, grinning all the while.

Dittmer chuckled, "You mock me?"

Touching her finger to her nose and pointing back at him, she gave him another wink.

As she reached for the door, he grabbed her one last time, pulling her in for another kiss. She was something different, and he loved every bit of her.

"I will keep you safe, my dear Thessaly," he said, crouching down in the shadows as she turned to open the door. *My dear Thessaly*, he thought.

CHAPTER 8

IT WAS STILL EARLY. The deck was empty, and the men slept. The only men up on deck were preoccupied with tasks. Thessaly beckoned Dittmer to come closer, putting her fingers to her lips, indicating he needed to be quiet. She pointed to the horizon where lightning flashed, long streaks running from cloud to cloud. A storm was brewing. This was not good. A storm could slow his brothers down or force them to change course. The time to act was now. They would have to be fast.

Dittmer slinked back into the hold, keeping the hatch open a crack to keep a close eye on Thessaly. She vanished out of his line of sight, and he worried, prepared to leap out and tear the heads off any man who had laid hands on her. He forced himself to wait and see what happened. He stood spying through the crack biting his lip and bouncing his knee anxiously. *This is taking too long. Something must have happened*, he thought. But just as he was about to burst through the door, Thessaly crept back inside.

"Here, wait for the sails to fall before you burst out. There are not many men on deck right now, but they will sound the alarm as soon as they realise what I'm doing." She said, handing him a small knife, a meat cleaver from the cook's private collection, along with a small axe. Lifting an eyebrow at her choice of weapons, he tucked the weapons into his boots and his belt. He looked up to see her dressing in clothes she had pilfered from somewhere. She stood proudly, looking every bit like a Viking warrior princess. His princess. His queen. His heart skipped a beat, and his groin twitched at the sight of her. He no longer cared that she was not Danish.

Not wanting to lose time before the storm hit, Thessaly crept out from the hold. This was no time for further words, even if she could think of what to say. Instead, she concentrated on the task at hand. If anyone spotted her, they would think she was just another of the Jarl's men.

In silence, she climbed the mast. Skilfully her fingers tugged at various threads. She was a skilled weaver, but even she knew the weak points in her work. She wrapped her legs tighter around the mast as the ship lurched in the wind. Looking out, she noticed how close the boat was to the others. She noted the direction of the current and waited a second. She was biding her time. A new plan began to form. She would slow down all three ships by crashing them into each other.

When she saw the distance between the ships close a little more as the wind grew stronger, she pulled the last thread. Like a crack in a frozen river, the threads detached from several parts of the sail, and shreds of fabric fell to the deck like leaves of a tree in Fall. Without the mainsail, the heavy winds caught in the few smaller sails, causing the ship to reel and turn, crashing into the other ship and forcing all three ships to become entangled.

At that moment a voice bellowed, sounding the alarm. As men leapt from their cabins, rushing to see what all the fuss was about, Dittmer jumped out from the hold like a monster from the deep, armed to the teeth. His axe in one hand and the butcher's knife in the other. Dittmer sliced through men with the fury of Asgärd as they came at him in droves. He tossed men overboard like they were rag dolls. They may have had the numbers, but they lacked Dittmer's fury and drive.

Seeing two men sneaking up behind Dittmer, Thessaly grabbed a rope from around the mast and swung down, kicking them hard as she barged into them, sending them flying overboard with loud cries of defeat.

Dittmer whirled to see what was going on and saw Thessaly taking a stand against a man who eyed her like she was a piece of meat. She pulled a small thin dagger from her waist. It reminded Dittmer of a sewing needle. it was so thin. But that didn't stop Thessaly from doing some damage with it. She was skilled in more ways than one. She dodged attacks almost as if she were dancing, and while the men she fought were distracted by her slinking movements and the sway of her hips, she used her needle-like dagger to slit throats and stab eyes.

My Greek Goddess, Dittmer thought, beaming with pride.

"I have another plan. I will be right back," she yelled over her shoulder to Dittmer. He glanced around, about to stop her from doing something foolish when she vanished below deck. Dittmer looked to the man Thessaly had slain and realised he wore the Keymaster's belt.

What is she planning? There was no time to ponder this further. Turning back to the men, he blocked attacks, crushing bones and sending men to their deaths at the bottom of the sea. The chaos of the incoming storm, the ships crashing into each other. The failing sails and the element of surprise. All these factors fell into place like pieces of a puzzle.

We can do this. Thessaly's plan is a success, Dittmer thought, hope swelling inside him. Behind him, he heard cheers and battle calls. Looking around, he couldn't see any other ships. Where could the sound be coming from?

Suddenly, a large group of shabby-looking men burst up from below deck carrying large wooden oars. *The rowers,* Dittmer thought. Thessaly burst through the crowd as they attacked Halfden's men, taking some of the pressure off Dittmer.

"You rallied the rowers?" he asked as she neared him.

She shook her head with a smile. "I freed the slaves and thralls. They deserve revenge for the loved ones they have lost at Halfden's hands," she said with pride and sorrow in her eyes.

Everything new he learned about this woman made him fall harder and harder for her.

"Look out!" she yelled as men swung across from the other ship. As the winds blew the vessels closer to each other, men climbed the masts slicing rope, trying to free themselves from the entanglement with the other ship. The ship tilted this way and that as the waves thrashed. Dittmer was steady on his feet, probably from spending most of his life at sea, but the Jarl's men didn't share that skill. As they wobbled and lost their footing, Dittmer, Thessaly, and the rowers continued their battle with increased success.

"Don't let him escape," one of the rower's voices yelled, pointing to the ship's side that began to separate from the other vessels. Thessaly and Dittmer followed the man's line of sight. The Jarl had managed to slip by unseen and leapt across to the other boat, swiftly followed by Njal. Dittmer charged towards them both, but the ship pulled away too quickly, widening the gap further than he could leap. Dittmer glared across as the Jarl waved back. His usual evil and twisted grin spread eye to eye.

How has he managed to escape again? Dittmer thought, slamming his fist against the ship's railing, screaming his frustration out across the sea.

CHAPTER 9

THUNDER ROARED AS LIGHTNING FLASHED, lighting up the sky. Rain fell hard and heavy, soaking everyone to the bone in moments. The fight grew tougher as the ships rocked unsteadily on the waves, and the ship's deck became slippery. Everyone struggled to keep their footing, slipping and sliding. Dittmer used this to his advantage, while Thessaly used the mast to gain height, swinging down and making good use of being able to attack from above.

"Ship ahead," yelled a distant voice from the Jarl's retreating ship. A new ship had appeared seemingly out of nowhere. The newcomer's ship sailed directly into the Jarl's ship, forcing him back and wedging him between the two.

"My brothers! I knew they would catch up." Dittmer cheered as he pulled his axe out of the chest cavity of a fallen man. His long thick hair clung to his face obscuring his view. He brushed it out of his face, to gain a clearer view of the ship.

Thessaly swung around the mast, her soaking wet hair blowing behind her in the wind, sending a chill through her bones. Clinging to rope with one hand, she sliced her needle-like blade through the neck of one of the Jarl's few remaining soldiers as she flew past and let go, landing gracefully in front of Dittmer.

Thessaly looked over to see men leaping from one ship to the other, ploughing through Halfden and his men with ease. Thessaly could see the family resemblance on the face of more than one giant. But what caught her eye most were the two women who fought with them. One looked like a noblewoman, but she brandished a bow just as well as any man. The other woman walked with a limp but didn't let it stop her. She occasionally leant on a man just as tall and intimidating as Dittmer, though he looked older.

"Who are they?" Thessaly asked, pointing to the two women, her eyes wide with admiration.

Dittmer let out a loud bellow of a laugh and shoved his axe high into the air, yelling an almost melodic battle cry. Two men stopped and turned, searching the ship for the origin of the sound. When they locked eyes on Dittmer, they raised their weapons above their heads and repeated the cry in wild delight.

"Not the brothers I thought would catch us. That's Abjörn and Erik. Back from Denmark!" He beamed, scooping Thessaly around the waist and jumping across to the other ship. Thessaly's stomach flipped as she feared he would drop her. She couldn't swim and feared drowning. But Dittmer would never let her fall, he held her tightly in his arms, and she loved how his muscled arms moulded to her form. *These arms were meant for me*, she thought as she leaned into his embrace.

With reinforcements, the odds were now even, and just as quickly as it began, the fight was over. Dittmer and his brothers cheered their victory, and the slaves and thralls on the ships cheered with them. They cheered even louder as Dittmer's brother, Abjörn, granted them all their freedom. The cheers swiftly turned to hisses of hatred and disdain. Dittmer's other brother, Erik, and his wife, Astrid, hauled a bound and gagged Jarl Halfden onto the deck.

"You will not escape this time, you traitorous snake. You will pay for your crimes," Abjörn bellowed.

Soaking wet from the storm, covered in the blood of the dead, you would think Thessaly would be freezing cold. But no, her blood ran warm, filled with adrenaline from the fight and lust for Dittmer. She had fought harder than she ever had – this was her first official battle, the first time she had to use the skills taught to her by her father. She wanted to impress Dittmer, but part of her wanted to protect him too. Seeing his manly form carve through his enemies like a knife through butter, seeing him help and protect the slaves who were too weak to fight; The images swam through her mind making her nipples into hard peaks through her soaked clothes. She wanted him like before; like that night they cuddled under his furs for warmth. But now, she was ravenous. She didn't just want him. She needed him.

"So, what happens now?" she asked.

Dittmer turned to her; his face was serious. He was next to her in two long strides, lifting her in his arms so she didn't have to hurt her neck looking up at him. He brought his lips down to hers without a word, and she returned the favour. There was something oddly titillating and intoxicatingly arousing about an imminent battle. They both felt it.

"Now, my sweet little Greek, we go home and punish the Jarl for his crimes," he said after breaking off their kiss.

She looked into his deep brown eyes. "…and then?"

He smiled and kissed her deeply once more, this time with more passion, and when he broke off their kiss, his eyes burned with hunger, a hunger for her.

"Then, my love, the world is ours," he breathed.

THE BROTHERS ARRIVED BACK at the settlement, meeting in the bay by the ship the other brothers had just launched to go after Dittmer. Together they returned to the settlement, triumphant and with much joy.

They were met with many cheers on their safe return. But joy changed to hisses and voices booming 'murderer' as Erik and Abjörn brought The Jarl up from the ship's hold. The entire settlement was ready for justice.

There were matters to settle. They all had things to discuss.

After locking the Jarl in the newly built prisoner's quarters, the brothers gathered with their wives in Abjörn's hut to plan what happened next.

"I would love nothing more than to run my sword through Beecham," Erik said, with a cautionary glance at Sima. She sat unfazed by his remark. She had started to harden when it came to her father. His crimes had removed any love she had for him. "But we must not do anything to start a war with the King of these lands. Beecham and the Jarl are one thing. We do not have the forces to battle the entire King's army," Erik continued.

"We also don't want him travelling to Denmark and continuing a war we started," Sören said.

The brothers looked around at each other, waiting for someone to figure out an answer to their conundrum. Beecham knelt in chains in the middle of the room. Dittmer stood over his shoulder, keeping guard, always with a close eye on Thessaly, who had easily taken to life in the settlement. Dittmer was happy to see how quickly his brother's wives accepted her.

Sima stepped forward, glaring down at her father.

"We put him back in what's left of Beecham castle...." She began, watching her father's eyes lighten up. He thought she was going to help him, but he was wrong. "As a prisoner," she continued.

Her father tried to jump to his feet, but Dittmer put a firm hand on his shoulder, keeping him in place.

"A prisoner in my own home? By my own blood?" he barked. Abjörn sat back, watching his beloved, knowing he didn't have to worry. She had proven she could take care of herself.

"At least you are a prisoner in your own home. You shipped me away. Isn't that right, father?" she asked coldly, kneeling to look at him dead in the eye. He wanted him to see the hurt and betrayal in her eyes. Beecham pressed his lips together. He couldn't exactly argue with this statement.

"Who will rule my castle if I am a prisoner?" he finally asked. Sima rose elegantly to her feet, a smile creeping up her face, as she glanced over to her husband. "The next heir," she began, flashing Abjörn a cheeky wink. "Me." She looked to her father, whose eyes were wide and jaw wide open in shock. "And my husband, of course."

Lord Beecham began to protest, but he quietened quickly when Sima pulled a knife and held it to his throat. Dittmer and Ryker escorted him back to the prisoner's quarters before returning to the next matter on the agenda. The Jarl. Dittmer and Ryker dragged

Halfden kicking and screaming into the hut, forcing him to his knees to answer the charges brought against him.

"Halfden, you must answer for your crimes," Abjörn began.

"You hired Beecham to kill our father. Do you deny it?" Abjörn boomed.

The Jarl didn't answer. He glared stone-faced, not wanting to incriminate himself any further.

"You plotted against our King. Do you deny it?" Abjörn asked, even louder this time as his patience wore thin. Once again, the Jarl said nothing. Instead, he spat at Abjörn's feet.

Ryker swung his arm and smacked Halfden around the back of the head.

"He can deny everything. He can even refuse to speak. But let's see what he has to say when witnesses to his crimes and admissions of guilt speak for you," Thessaly said. Dittmer's face beamed with pride at how she stood defiant in the face of the man who once traded her like she was nothing more than a piece of meat.

Thessaly addressed the room. "I have several fellow slaves who have proof of your crimes against their father and your King. I also have a witness who talks of your involvement in the demise of the King's sons," she said.

The hut erupted in chatter. Dittmer looked over at her, confused. She had not mentioned this information before.

"Lies," The Jarl boomed before Dittmer smacked him upside the head again.

"You are so cocky, bragging about your actions. You think slitting the throats and burying bodies keeps your confessions hidden. But no, loyalty is an illusion. People only stay loyal while you hold a purpose to their needs," she said, and the realisation hit the Jarl like a hammer to the head.

"No! you turned Njal?" Halfden asked, fear spiking through him as sweat beaded on his brow.

"Oh yes. When faced with losing his life, be begged for mercy and offered you up on a silver platter to save his neck," Thessaly finished in triumph.

They had all they needed: witnesses, a plan for keeping their new home safe, and a way to finally get justice for their father. Halfden would have to travel back to Denmark to face the King's wrath.

"So, it is settled. Erik and Dittmer will travel back to Denmark and present the Jarl and Njal to the King to answer for their crimes. Thessaly, will you travel with my brother? Will you take the slaves you speak off?" Abjörn asked, holding out his hand for her to take. She wrapped her small hand around his sizeable bulking forearm and nodded.

"The slaves, will they be freed?" she asked tentatively.

"They are slaves no longer," Abjörn finished, and Thessaly let out a breath she had not realised she was holding.

The brothers embraced before heading out for the evening. The day had been tiresome, and rest was needed for the journey ahead. Abjörn and Sima would prepare to take Beecham Castle, with a plan of rebuilding it to even greater heights than it had ever been previously, leaving Sören and Firtha to lead the settlement. Erik and Dittmer would travel to Denmark and Ryker. Well, Ryker had relaxed since the Jarl and Beecham's fates had been sealed. He was back to his childish joking self. He agreed Sören would need help running the settlement since the birth of his son.

"We will see each other again, brothers. This is not the end of our journey together," Abjörn said. They all departed, heading off to get a good night's rest, conflicted by their feelings. They were sad to be parting once again but happy that their war was finally over, and justice was being served for their father. Dittmer had no doubt in his mind that he and his brothers would meet again soon. He knew if word got out that one was in need, the others would travel from all the corners of the world to be by their side. To help. To protect. And to fight for glory.

CHAPTER 10

As Thessaly and Dittmer strolled back to his hut, Thessaly looked around in wonder. She could see why he had fought so valiantly for this place. Love filled the air, the love of family, friends, and community. People happily helped each other and took pride in their homes. As she watched a young woman embrace her father, her heart ached. She missed her family. She had stopped thinking about them long ago, as the memory was too painful. *Were they safe? Were they alive?* She didn't know, but she longed to.

"You look sad. What's wrong?" Dittmer asked as they entered his small hut. He cradled her face in his arms and wiped away a stray tear with his thumb. She turned her face and planted a gentle kiss on his palm.

"This place has just got me thinking. I can see why you and your brothers fought so hard to preserve this place. I can feel the love and friendship radiating off everyone. This settlement is truly a home," she said, cutting herself off as she felt a lump form in her throat.

"You miss your home?" Dittmer asked. He could feel his heart breaking at the thought of losing her to lands far away.

She shook her head gently. "Not home. My family. I haven't allowed myself to think of them for the longest time. It hurts too much. But after tonight, I wish I knew if they were safe," she answered, crumbling into Dittmer's embrace.

As someone who had lost his father, he understood her pain. The not knowing, the doubting. Such a thing was soul-crushing. He held her tight to him. He would not be so selfish as to stop her from travelling home. If her happiness meant he would lose her, that would be a pain he would live with.

But then an idea popped into his head.

"We travel to Denmark in the morn. Once the Jarl has answered for his crimes, we do not have to come back to these shores," he said.

Pulling away and looking up at him, Thessaly's heart began to race. She didn't want to allow herself to hope.

"Once we have finished with the King's business, we can take a ship and find your family," Dittmer said. Thessaly's eyes brimmed with tears. Her smile was brighter than the moon in the night sky.

"Do you mean it?" she asked, holding her hand over her heart as if shielding it.

"Yes, I know the pain of losing family and being apart from the ones you love. I do not want to be apart from you, you are free, and I want to make you smile every day. After Denmark, we travel to Greece," he said.

Thessaly leapt into his arms and wrapped hers so tightly around his neck Dittmer worried she might cut off his breath.

"I have never been in love before, but there is no other way to describe how I feel about you," Thessaly whispered as she landed a kiss of fierce passion on Dittmer's lips.

Pushing herself out of his embrace, she took his hand and led him to the cot in the corner. She pushed him gently, and he sat down, looking her over as she stood in front of him.

"I am willing, are you?" she asked with lust-filled eyes and a mischievous glint in her eyes.

Dittmer nodded with a chuckle. She pulled her dress down her shoulders and stepped out of her clothes. Dittmer stood, unable to take his eyes off her. He circled her slowly, running his fingers over her stomach and hips. Her skin was beautiful and soft, like silk. Her buttocks was round and firm. Her breasts stood proudly upon her chest, and her nipples peaked as he touched her. Stopping in front of her, he brought his lips down to hers as he ran a hand up her thigh and played with the small, neat mound of hair guarding the place he longed to touch the most.

Not removing her lips from his, Thessaly ran her hands up to unclip his furs. Dittmer's skin tingled as her fingers traced his body, undressing him. Breaking off their embrace, Thessaly kissed his collar bone, standing on her tiptoes to reach. She trailed kisses down his solid form. Taking his nipple in her mouth, she rolled her tongue over his chest, and Dittmer let his head fall back, sucking in a short breath. She continued to explore his torso with her trail of kisses. She dropped to her knees, seductively running her tongue over her lips as she locked eyes with him. Gently, she took his shaft in her mouth, taking him deeper and caressing him with her tongue.

Dittmer had never felt pleasure like it before. His knees went weak. Gripping him with her hand, she stroked him even as her mouth pleasured him.

"Oh, Thess...." he started, the pleasure she gave him rendering him unable to speak even her name. She picked up speed, and Dittmer saw stars flashing in his eyes; she was spectacular. "Wait," he managed to say, even if it was barely a squeak.

Thessaly let him go and rose to her feet. He spun her around and sat her on the bed without saying a word. He wanted to taste her how she had tasted him. He spread her legs wide and trailed kisses along her inner thigh, kisses everywhere but the part which needed kissing the most.

He could tell she wanted it, and he enjoyed teasing her. She opened her mouth to speak his name when he wrapped his mouth around her, sucking at the tender bud between her legs.

He felt her tremble at his touch. Her breathing increased as his tongue teased her. Waves of pleasure took over her as she felt her climax growing. He wanted to hear her scream with pleasure. Dittmer spread her lips and plunged his fingers deep, covering himself in her sweet nectar. With his other hand, he reached up and cupped her breast. It fit his hand perfectly.

"Dittmer.... Dittmer," she began to pant as her fingers entwined with his hair. He felt her grip tighten as she arched her back and screamed out in ecstasy as her body trembled with the pleasure that rose like fire in her veins.

"I'm not finished with you yet." Dittmer grinned as he brought his mouth to her breast, then kissed her deeply. She could taste her pleasure on his tongue, and it sent the fire of desire running through her.

"Good." She grinned as she fell back on the bed, eager for him to take her.

He couldn't hold back any longer. He had felt how tight she was with his fingers. He had tasted her sweetness. He needed to feel her around him. In one swift motion, he entered her, and they both moaned in pleasure. They fit together perfectly. He stretched her, and she clenched around him. Thessaly wrapped her legs around his waist and gripped his shoulders as he began slowly moving in and out of her.

As their pleasure grew, their moans matched each other. While making love was hot, heavy, and beautiful, Thessaly needed more. She had wanted him since they cuddled in the hold. She had wanted him more as she watched him in battle, and she needed him more than ever.

"Take me like you would a Viking woman," she whispered in his ear.

"Are you sure?" he asked with a wicked grin.

She nodded, nipping him on his earlobe to punctuate just how much she wanted this.

His thrusts grew stronger and faster, the sound of their bodies colliding, and their moans of pleasure filled the hut. It was not long before Thessaly felt her climax build again. But this was with an intensity she had never experienced. It overtook her sending her vision white as she shook under Dittmer. She arched her back as she felt his ecstasy meet hers.

They crumbled around each other, Dittmer coming to rest his head on Thessaly's chest, listening to her heart pound as they caught their breaths. Their sweat-covered bodies wrapped around each other.

"You are mine now, Dittmer," she breathed, kissing his forehead and playing with his long sweat-soaked hair.

"And you are mine, my sweet, beautiful Thessaly," he groaned, as he pulled her close, sleep taking the both of them into dreams of the future that was to be theirs.

THE END

Did you enjoy *The Jürgensen Vikings*?
Please consider reviewing it on Goodreads, Bookbub, or your favorite retailer! Reviews help me reach new readers.

Read The King's Raiders

www.ingramcontent.com/pod-product-compliance
Lightning Source LLC
Chambersburg PA
CBHW031400250626
47155CB00004B/1339